Books by Raven McAllan

Diomhair

Secrets Shared
Secrets Uncovered
Secrets Remembered
Secrets Dispatched
Secrets Learned
Secrets Dispelled

Single Titles

Hong Kong Heat
Taken Identity
Fairground Attraction

Fairground Attraction

ISBN # 978-1-78686-094-1

©Copyright Raven McAllan 2016

Cover Art by Posh Gosh ©Copyright 2016

Interior text design by Claire Siemaszkiewicz

Totally Bound Publishing

Published in 2016 by Totally Bound Publishing, Newland House, The Point, Weaver Road, Lincoln, LN6 3QN, United Kingdom.

FAIRGROUND ATTRACTION

RAVEN MCALLAN

Dedication

To Debra. Thank you for your support and our wine
awaydays.
To Ann for such great editing
And to Paul as ever. Love you x

Chapter One

Tinny music blared from all directions, multicolored lights flickered, teenagers shrieked, pushing past families and older couples arm in arm. Generators — their cables snaking across the ground, ready to trip up the unwary — added noise, plus their particularly oily smell, to the other odors of grease and popcorn. All the fun of the fair. He loved it. Every last screaming child or puking teen. Each was a part of the whole.

His world. Even if he had to leave it and go back to his other life soon, for now this was all he wanted.

Raig stood and watched the crowds, always on the alert for anything untoward. Kids on their dad's shoulders, mums pushing prams, couples holding hands as they decided where to go and what to do. A group of teenage boys, all swagger and bravado, stalked by and similar groups of giggling girls nudged and shoved one another. A normal evening at the fair.

He got the odd admiring glance, and ignored it. Something he found easy to do. One couple in particular caught his eyes. They were resolutely dragging an older woman in his direction. She looked as if she'd prefer root canal treatment. *Ah, show time. Suck it up, Raig.* Whether he liked it or not, a promise was just that — a promise. He didn't make many, but those he did, he honored.

"Come on." He heard Lorna, the younger woman, urging the older lady. He looked down at the other lady's feet to see them encased in sensible ballet flats, albeit with something sparkly across the toes. *Go figure. Semi-sensible then.*

He glanced up at her face and his heart missed a beat.

More than just a beautiful woman, she reached out to his soul, making him ache to know her in every way. *What the fuck?* That jolt of recognition, the electricity in his body, scared him. Was this what his da had meant? Recognizing a woman as his? *Shit, if it were a film, the violins would be playing.*

He'd always thought that his da had just been fanciful, making up the love-at-first-sight thing because it sounded so romantic and made his mum laugh, blush and poke Da in the ribs. Now? Well, now he wondered if maybe all those romance writers had hit the nail on the head. Shit, never mind the nail, he felt as if *he* had been hit on the head. With a sledgehammer. Him, a normally straightforward, hard-talking, no-nonsense businessman, thinking of roses and champagne, soft music and…yeah, and sex. Okay, so the sex bit was normal, the rest wasn't.

"Mum, stop lagging."

Mum? Oh fucking shit. This vibrant, sexy woman was Vairi, Lorna's mum? The woman he was going to give a good time? *Whew, 'give a good time' just took on a whole new meaning.* It was unfortunate, but he suspected it was not the one Lorna and Denny wanted him to give her. The woman sighed deeply.

"I need to lag. You go on without me. I'll sit and…smell the daisies."

Raig chuckled. The stare she gave him should have withered his balls. He winked. She scowled, leaned on one of the security fences around the galloping horses and looked in the other direction.

"What shall we go on first?" Lorna shouted, her voice pitched above the noise. She sounded eager as she looked toward the chair-o-planes, the longing expression on her face there for everyone to see. The older woman rolled her eyes, raised her eyebrows and took a deep breath before exhaling heavily.

"You two can go on that torture ride. I'll be here watching you and not losing my tea."

Time to make his presence felt. He moved closer to her. "Ah, pretty lady. Sure, you'll not lose your tea, but you can't be at the fair and not have a ride."

She whirled around, her long curls — the color of a raven's wing — flipping across his face. He saw chagrin in her eyes and something else. Attraction? He and his ever-tightening body hoped so. His mind went to those classic novels his sisters had force-fed him. *Lady Chatterley's Lover, Wuthering Heights, The Story of O.* Okay, that wasn't a classic per se, but he could imagine them both in it. He wondered what she saw when she looked at him. Six foot three tall. Inky, almost black eyes, overlong, dark, curly hair, one earring. Tattoos almost hidden with just one tantalizing bird's wing showing. Tanned and toned.

He chuckled as she put her nose in the air, but not before she stared at him as if to reach into his soul. The sort of stare he would bet had nailed lesser men than him to the floor and kept them there and reduced them to babbling wrecks before they slunk away defeated. Not him.

His tone teased, low and husky as he leaned in a little closer. "So, what will your pleasure be?"

Did he really hear her say, 'You naked'?

"Pardon?" *Say that again.*

"I'm sorry I need to go." Pure frost. "My son-in-law is waiting for me."

His smile was, with a bit of luck, wickedness personified. "I see him." He raised his voice to be heard over a distorted rendition of *Greased Lightnin'*. Even John Travolta had trouble beating a fairground's volume. "Are you well then, Denny?" He waved. "I have her. You and your lovely lady have a good evening now. As we will." A laugh, a wave, a swift hug of her shoulders. "Now then, Lorna's mum. What will be your pleasure?"

Vairi rolled her eyes. "For you to cut the crap and that phony Irish accent, to be sure." She mimicked him. "'Tis as fake as that Rolex you're wearing. Own up to whatever shit you and your co-conspirators have thought up, find me a taxi and pay for the bloody thing." There was the stare again. "Give me a break and don't follow their well-meaning but unwelcome footsteps and try to" — she mimed quote marks — "make sure I have a good time, and show me what I'm missing. Seriously, I'm happy with my life and would be a lot happier without well-intentioned people trying to change it," she finished with a snap. "So thanks but no thanks whatever you're about to suggest. Unless it's to escort me to the taxi rank."

Oh ho, feisty. "Ouch. Oh, *a chuisle*, you pain me, indeed you do." Did he sound as wounded as he felt? "Not shit at all. The Rolex is as real as those deep blue eyes of yours."

"Bugger."

Her stern expression relaxed and he swore he could see how she fought with herself not to give in to humor. Hopefully she wasn't so annoyed as she'd tried to project.

"Now if only I could say I wore colored lenses. However, like George Washington, I cannot tell a lie. So Mister…"

"O'Shea. Padraig O'Shea. And you?" He bent over her hand and kissed it. A soft kiss, full of promise. Theatrical, but what the hell, he meant it. He, who had always steered clear of commitment, of ladies who clung, demanded attachment and wanted more than this. He had no idea why, how or when. Just that he did. Her laughter surprised and delighted him.

"Vairi McQueen." Her voice held an absent tone. "Oh my God. Never. Paddy O'Shea. Next you'll be telling me 'indeed and there's a leprechaun on my shoulder'."

He contrived to look wounded. "Never, ever would I be joking about leprechauns, lovely lady. Also, no, I'm not Paddy O'Shea."

"Told you." She huffed, her eyes glittering in triumph. "I knew it. Lies, all lies. So who are you?"

"Paddy O'Shea is my da," he continued as if she hadn't spoken. "I'm Raig."

"Rake? That sounds about right." She shook her head. "I don't half get them. Any oddball or weirdo and they come my way. And there's something else. How do you know Denny?"

He chose to ignore her. "Now, I cannot be escorting a lovely lady and be calling her 'Lorna's mum'. I'll be calling you Vairi My Queen."

She glared. "You're not escorting me anywhere long enough for that."

"Now that's where you're wrong, love. God knows what's in the water around here, but I can't help it." He bent his head and kissed her cheek, hoping to hell he wouldn't end up with a black eye for his trouble. "You've bewitched me."

Vairi shook her head. "You're well-named, Rake O'Shea."

In reply, he put his arms under hers and swung her around until the lights swirled. As he slowed she staggered and he held her close for a second, liking the way she felt as she rested against him. "How's your dinner?"

"Bastard. My stomach wishes it had never met you. I can't say it's a pleasure to have done so."

He could. *His* stomach was so churned up, a brass band could had taken up residence and was fighting the fairy folk for space. She was all woman, and his gut told him she should be all *his* woman. There was no rhyme or reason, just a certain 'this is it, I've found her' feeling. Something he accepted did happen to people, but never to him — until that moment. "Well then, Vairi My Queen. Tonight is yours. Requested, arranged and plotted by Lorna, who says you don't get out enough. Denny and I were at school together, almost six months of every year when the fair overwintered. He knew I'd be more than happy to escort a lovely lady and show her the…sights." It might have started as a favor to someone who'd helped him out of more scrapes than anyone could imagine, but now? *Oh now, thank you, Denny!*

She waited, and watched him with close attention. He had no idea why. Her reaction was most perplexing. If he wasn't mistaken though, Lorna and Denny would get a piece of her mind when she saw them next, which left him wondering what would be her follow-up move.

"All mine? To choose or discard things?" she asked and licked her lips.

Oh fuckety fuck. His dick tried to thrust through denim. Sweet lord, did she *know* what that did to him?

"Use or loose as I please? And you'll not argue?"

Shit. "I'll try not to," he said honestly. "I'm not saying I'll succeed."

"Honesty. I like that."

She did that bloody arousing lick over her lips again.

"Okay then. The galloping horses. Then the big wheel." She laughed up at him. "A hot dog and onions and some candy floss. So, Rake, you game?"

"Oh, Vairi My Queen, more than game. A woman after my own heart."

She giggled. "That's one thing I'm not. After your heart," she elaborated as he stared at her blankly. "I have enough trouble with mine, let alone anyone else's. I'm just after your fairground rides for a wee while."

Raig tucked his arm inside hers and executed a mock bow as he led her across the grass toward the ride she'd requested. "That can be arranged. Let's go." He interspersed the short walk with a few words of caution—'mind the cable now' and 'sure, and don't be falling over the bin'.

As he was at least seven or eight inches taller than her, Raig found it easy to maneuver Vairi tight up against him, as he enjoyed her subtle scent and feeling her soft body next to his. If he had his way, there'd be a lot more feeling and soon. It was a strange sensation. Usually he kept his distance with any woman. With his other employment it paid not to have anyone around who the alleged opposition could use as leverage. Raig was invisible and intended he and his stayed that way.

So, no long term lovers.

Oh, he'd enjoyed his share of affairs, but no one had managed to get through his social mask and into his mind. Until now.

When they reached the side of the first ride, he turned

her into his arms and lifted her effortlessly onto one of the painted horses before he stepped up after her.

"Now then, that's you seated on Sword." Oh, so aptly named. With luck, he'd have her seated on *his* sword before long. "Scoot forward so there's room for me tucked in behind you."

He imagined his eyes twinkled and dared her to disagree, as she scowled and rose to the challenge.

"Oh, Mr. Rake, I'll *show* you. I may be way into my forties, but hey, I can flirt and enjoy, *if* I can remember how to do it."

Interesting. She looked about thirty. Impossible, he knew, if she was truly Lorna's mum. "So, how old are you?"

Vairi narrowed her eyes, very wary and on the defensive. "Why does it matter?" Her tone was full of suspicion. "Is there an upper age limit to riding these things?"

"It doesn't matter as far as I'm concerned. I'm just a nosy bugger. I go by the adage, you're as old as the person you feel." He smirked and hoped she would get the allusion to his age and the possibility she would be touching *him*. To make sure, he took her hand and placed it on his chest. The warmth of her touch hit him even through his shirt. If the material had scorched, he wouldn't have been surprised. "Now think on, I'm thirty-one. Therefore, by that rule, QED, so are you."

"Fuck." She snatched her hand back as if she'd been stung, and shook her head. "Sod it. If you're that age, that makes me almost old enough to be your mother. And if it works both ways, *you'll* be feeling geriatric."

Raig roared with laughter and gave in to the impulse to peck her on the cheek again. "Nah. It matters not. You are what you are. Which is perfect for me. So, Vairi My Queen, ready to roll?" He swung onto the horse behind her, moving her forward until she was stopped by the pole, which he imagined was tight between her legs and rubbed up against her pussy. When they began to move it should be more than arousing for her. And agony to watch and not participate for him. Raig's cock strengthened, lengthened and hardened against her. Would she complain? Or comply and lean back into him? He had no idea. She wriggled and moaned softly under her breath as his dick did its best to chisel into her ass.

Steady. At least she didn't turn around and thump him.

All he could do was to try to arrange things in his favor. Raig bent into her and whispered, "Ah, Vairi My Queen, this is what you do to me. Giving me such a hard-on, I'm wanting to bury myself far inside you, so deep, until you cry out my name in passion. But until you're happy with the idea, we'll be riding the horses." Oh, how he wished he were a mind reader. Judging by the look he saw on her face as the mirrors on the ride flashed by, maybe it was a good idea he wasn't. Had he gone too far too fast? Ah well, he'd rather be open and honest than coy and calculating.

Nodding at Jonny, a tall, skinny, blond-headed man who was in charge of the roundabout, Raig held Vairi firm as the ride quickened, each horse going up and down to its own pattern. As the roundabout began to speed up even further, he felt Vairi stiffen and hold on to the pole so tight her knuckles were white. *Why the hell did she choose the ride if it upset her so?* Unless the hardness of the pole on her pussy was worth it. So he would make sure the sensation of his cock crowding her ass surpassed anything else she may feel. From the subtle shift of her hips, he could tell how turned on she was. Well, fuck, if the pole did the job, who was he to complain? He could replace those emotions later.

He said softly, "Sway with the motion, move with it. That's good." He encouraged her as they spun around, lights blurring together, music flowing from one ride to another. A good thing about being the boss—they could stay where they were for as long as they liked. Raig could sense her becoming aroused. Her breathing changed pace and her body shook as the friction between him and the ride increased and intensified.

"Fuck you, Raig. This is so not me," she said shakily as her skin flushed and the silken sheen of arousal slicked over it.

"Why not, love? Just let go."

"I can… I can't not… Oh shit…" Vairi leaned back into him before she shuddered and shivered her climax. Fuck it, how he wished he could have seen her face as she came.

The roundabout began to slow for the third—or was it fourth—time. Raig pressed gentle kisses along her neck. "I need to be an active worker for this go around. I'll be back before you know it, well before your ride has finished. I need to help Jonny there to collect the fares." He moved away, with reluctance, and off the horse. "I need to be with you. Hell, I'm needy."

"Ditch the accent," she said huskily. "Be natural." 'Or else' was the inference.

"Ah, Vairi My Queen. It's mine," he said easily. "God's truth. My voice. The voice I'll use as I make love with you."

Nimbly, he moved away before she could reply, swaying easily as the motion of the ride picked up once more. Raig glanced over at Vairi and frowned. Was it a case of once around too often? *My, she does look pale.* He could only hope she didn't toss her cookies until he was able to get her off. He motioned to Jonny to go to her and check on how she was coping.

Raig took up the fare from three squealing teenagers and sensed Vairi's eyes on him. He noticed her wan smile in response to Jonny, as he spoke to her. As soon as all the fares were in, the ride would stop. *Why on earth did she ask to go on something she couldn't handle? Women. Would any man ever understand them?* One minute he was watching her come, the next about to throw up. *Mind you, four rides on the trot probably was a tad excessive.*

As the ride slowed, he made his way back to her. "Now then, Vairi My Queen. You're looking green. Ah, you've made me a poet, sure I didn't know it."

"You oaf," she said thickly. "Think yourself lucky I didn't thump you. Please, please, get me off this ride. Sheesh, what planet am I on? Wherever, I've left my common sense behind, that's for sure. I hate bloody things that go round. Oh hell, help me off now, pretty damn quick, or I'll be sick. Oh fuck, you've got me doing it now."

Watching her face, it was easy to worry. "Ah, love. It's stopping. There now, I'll get you down. Whoa, let me do the work." She slumped against him. "That's my girl." Gently he lifted her off the ride. He was sure if she hadn't felt so ill, she would have been embarrassed.

Worry churned Raig's gut. He had entered into the spirit of the evening reasonably uninvolved. He had agreed to help Denny and Lorna out when they had requested he entertain Vairi for a while, as he knew he would be at a loose end during the early hours of the fair's opening. He was the boss man. The one to wander around and keep an eye out for anything and everything, but he wouldn't be the only one doing that.

I'm the spare part, really. Some saw him as a part-timer who played at the fair. Raig knew he didn't and spent as much time there as humanly possible. What some people didn't understand, was if he didn't do other work—even though they weren't told exactly what—the fair wouldn't be as it was. Takings never covered the running costs. His alter ego was needed, even if it was a yoke around his neck at times.

Raig understood Lorna's worries, had heard how she felt all her mum did was work and garden. How she never went out and enjoyed herself. He knew if it had been his mum, he'd want her to have a life as fulfilled and interesting as possible as well. And, he'd reasoned, all they wanted from him was a few hours of his time. Not much to ask of a good friend. However, it seemed, after he'd looked into a pair of dark blue eyes and watched the bravado there, he'd gone from fancy-free to entwined in thirty seconds flat.

It didn't scare him. That was a first. Raig had always thought of commitment as akin to the plague. To be feared and avoided like, well, the plague.

Now this gorgeous woman with a slim body, legs encased in deep navy denim that seemed to go up to her ears, breasts that would be—he was sure—the perfect handful and a smile to launch ships, had him aroused in seconds. Her eyes were, he decided stupidly, liquid pools to drown in, and her loose gray blouse hinted at mysteries to be found. Although the sallowness of her skin and the misery in those eyes had him worried, he was still hot, horny and hard. Signaling to Jonny he was going, he lifted Vairi tight into his arms and carried her through the crowds to his trailer.

He could no more ignore the elegant line of her neck than stop breathing. It invited soft, nipping kisses. Fuck, he knew she was suffering, but he was suffering, too, though not with motion sickness, more like with lack of motion. Of the in-out variety.

She moaned softly in his arms. Ah, shit, Denny would kill him. After Lorna had. In his defense, no one had thought to tell him she got motion sick. What exactly had they imagined they would be doing all evening? Playing bingo, for fuck's sake? He had more than an idea what he would like to be doing with Vairi. Somehow he didn't think Lorna would have the *same* idea.

In his arms, Vairi struggled to sit up. "What the hell?" she asked huskily and coughed. "What was that?"

Well, that was spoken loud and clear, at any rate. "Hush now. You were feeling not so well on the ride. I'm taking you somewhere private and quiet to rest a while."

"White slaving?" The chuckle, although weak, was definitely there. "Toss your cookies to be taken?"

Ah, that deserved a kiss—this one on her forehead. Christ, when was he going to bite the bullet and kiss her, firm and possessive, on the mouth? When she didn't look as if she was going to pass out. Or throw up on him.

"If that's what you're wanting. If not, just to my trailer until you don't look the same color as that lovely blouse you are wearing." He smiled at her nod. "Seriously, I was worried."

"And me. I've not been that bad before. I wanted to die."

"You and me both, love, you and me both," he said

fervently. Raig skirted the big wheel and took care not to trip over the trailing cables before he walked quickly toward a large olive-green caravan. "Hold on a sec." He mounted the steps and held her steady while he fumbled in his pocket to find the key. "Can you stand a moment as I unlock the door?" Damn, he was losing the brogue. Even though it might not be needed, as camouflage it was good enough. Did he still need to hide who he was? He had no idea. *Think, Raig.* "Yeah?"

She nodded again. "Think so."

"There's a girl. Be holding on to me now." With care, he set her down on the top step and unlocked the door, propelled her in and helped her to sit on a long, comfy bench settee. "Now then, my brave one, I'm thinking a cup of tea might just help."

"No, honestly, I'm fine now. A glass of water, then I'll get something to eat." She blushed, and nibbled her bottom lip. "Like I said, I'm not usually anywhere near that bad. No dinner combined with the trauma of being abandoned by my family might have a lot to do with it."

"Ah, well, I'll be thinking most people would be affected that way." He poured a glass of water as he spoke. Vairi took it with a murmur of thanks and sipped slowly. Then she nodded, put the half-full glass down on a side table and cleared her throat. Unease traveled through him at the look of determination on her face.

Uh-oh. It was the universal 'cut the crap, ditch the shit and open up and be honest' look so many women had down to perfection. Usually it annoyed him, this time it worried him. *Fuck, I have it bad.*

"Right then, Rake O'Shea. Gloves-off time. Who are you, why do you keep using that phony accent, and what the hell is going on?" Vairi demanded in a tone sharp enough to split logs. "No bullshitting me, or this water might find its way to your face."

Hell on wheels. He winced as he realized he had to think on his feet. Fast. Jeez, that sexy shoe was tapping on the floor and those glittery things that decorated it caught the light as she moved. *Cool it, Raig. Concentrate. Use your brains not your balls.* Not easy when said balls vied with his cock over which was the hardest. It was a close-run thing and walking would soon be difficult without emulating John Wayne.

"My name is Padraig O'Shea," Raig said carefully. "I have known Denny since we were young. He and the lovely Lorna asked for my help. I wasn't going to say no. I'm bloody glad I didn't."

"How young?" Vairi ignored the latter part of his statement and picked up her glass again. He eyed it warily. "Define young," she added.

Hell, that voice could break eggs. Bite the bullet, Raig, you're not going to wriggle out of this. "He was five, I was seven. So I'll do the maths for you in case you've forgotten how. I'm thirty-one. Born in Dublin. Single, solvent and clean. My da always was working with the fair. He met my ma when it was set up there. He said it was love at first sight for him, but it took her a while to believe him. Married thirty-five years and as daft for each other now as they ever were."

"'Was' as in not now?" Of course she'd pick up on the 'was', being as she was no slouch in the brains department. Her erotic, foot-tapping rhythm said 'take me, fuck me' and was making him hot as it sent messages from his brain to his cock and back again. Those sodding, fecking arousing scenarios were playing havoc with his concentration. What was he supposed to be answering? *Oh fuck, Da and the fair.*

"Ah well, Vairi My Queen, that's the rub. Sometimes, although now more for the *craic* than the necessity." Why did the look she was giving him have him wanting to cover all the strategic parts of his body? "Otherwise he's at home with my ma and playing lord of the manor, so he is."

"For fuck's sake, cut the crap." The water in her glass rippled violently as she slammed it down. She stood and paced across the trailer before swinging to face him, her hair following the motion in a forceful sweep across her face.

Ah, that was why his hands, hovering over his cock and balls, were ready to take evasive action — her frustration was palpable.

"I, ah… Okay, tell me what you want," he said slowly, his mind racing. "And I'll do my best."

"Please, Padraig. Okay, I'll accept I've been set up," she said in an exasperated voice. "Now I know why Lorna was so insistent I came to the fair with her and Denny. She knows I don't do rides well. But what exactly was I set up for? Surely my daughter wasn't pushing me toward an evening of sex and satisfaction?"

Laughing at the look of horror on her face as she realized what she had said, he made to reassure her. "No, no, Vairi My Queen, that was not in her mind." *It is in my mind though. Oh, by God, is it in my mind.* "I was out with the two of them on Tuesday, and Lorna was saying that you'd been commenting you were in a rut and needed get out or drown in wallowing crappiness. Her words, not mine. She wanted to help you — all work and no play is not good. So I said if they brought you with them tonight, I'd show you a good time. I wasn't thinking you would go a strange shade of gray when I did."

That elicited a reluctant laugh. "Okay, I concede that's my own fault. I decided to jump out of my rut. I forgot the parachute. Hell, I should know better. I even get motion sick in the passenger seat of a car. Should have stuck to hook-a-duck."

He chuckled with her. "Would looking at the water round those cute little ducks not be making you seasick then?"

"Jeez, Rake, drop the accent, why don't you. You keep dipping in and out so much I'm giddy. It's not real, it's phony. You sound like a stereotypical B-movie. Yes?"

He shook his head as he looked at her and replied with not entirely faked sorrow. "That's where you are wrong. I'll admit I've been piling it on. Lorna said you were a romantic, inspired by sexy accents, and as I've been told over the years, the Irish accent is just that, sexy, so I thought, well, why not? To be honest and truthful, the lilt is always there. It's just been weakened over the years. I resurrected it for you." He watched her, as she seemed to mull over his statement. He could imagine her dissecting every word and pulling up to consider the bits she chose to.

"I'll buy into that. Right." She took a deep breath and smiled. A look hot enough to split his jeans if he wasn't careful. A lesser expression than that had started wars, he was certain.

"So, Rake." The way she purred his name sent his libido sky high, and he swore there would be a stain on the cloth. "A good name, by the way. Now, what *are* you going to show me?"

His cock understood what he wanted. It was hard and tight up against the fly of his denims, straining the zip in its effort to be free of its confines. He was glad Mr. Levi Strauss knew a thing or two about the strength of that particular cloth.

"It depends on how much you want to fly." His accent was now upper-class English. "I have an idea about what I'd like." He saw her considering his statement. "I'll be open and honest. I agreed at first because of a photo in Lorna's purse. The pair of you, somewhere sunny."

"Barbados," Vairi said, her voice faint. "Three years ago, just before she married. It was my birthday present. We ate, drank and sunbathed. No sex." She giggled. "Lord that sounds icky. I mean neither of us went off and had sex with anyone."

"Shame." He laughed. "Does your daughter not understand you are a living, breathing, sexy woman?"

She laughed with him. "Probably not. No girl or woman or, I suspect, male likes to think their mother knows about, you know, sex. Okay, we've had the kids, but then? Zilch. Won't they be in for a surprise when they get to that state?"

He nodded and decided to use the element of surprise to catch her off guard. "So, Vairi My Queen, did you come on the horse? With its rod pressed hard where my cock wanted to be?" He took a gamble and guessed—hoped—she wouldn't be shocked or offended by his frank speech. Vairi blushed, but no angry words accompanied it. So far, so good. Now he intended to make her less self-conscious.

"I could have done," Raig remarked frankly. "Very easily. Hard up against your ass, with you rubbing against me and that bloody pole. Knowing it gave you more of a good time than my cock was gutting. *Gutting*. What I really wanted was my cock in you, never mind the pole. I would be your pole. Hot, hard, and fuck you into oblivion. Hear you come. Feel you come. That's what I want. To feel you milk me to fruition."

"Ah..." She seemed to struggle for an answer. Vairi stroked her index finger across his cheek and seared a line down to his lips, which she tapped twice. "So? Why are you waiting? Be that pole, Rake. Because all I thought about as I got hot and bothered was you. You inside me, making me come. Now's your chance. If you're not worried how old I am, why should I be? Cougars of the world unite and all that. Show me how you're going to fuck me, Rake. Show me what you want, how you want it. Let me shout and scream for you."

He was nonplussed. Of anything he'd hoped she say, that went over and above it. Boy, she surprised him. Big time.

"Love." He had what he wanted, and now he was hesitating. *What the fuck? Get real, Raig.* "Are you sure, Vairi? God, I want you, do I ever. I want to hear you moan, see you writhe as I fill you and fuck you hard. Make you come as you scream my name. But I don't want you to be wishing we hadn't, come tomorrow."

She sniggered. "That statement could be taken two ways. I'll not wish I hadn't come, come tomorrow, I promise."

He smiled. *Trust her.* "Good but, love, listen well. It'll mark you. Make you mine. I'll bite, nip and scar. I'll take you. Brand you. I may have only known you for a few hours, but by God, I know the type of man I am. If I make you mine, it'll be forever. I know my own mind, I have faith in my intuition, and it's letting me know this is 'it'. So think very carefully, my Vairi. Are you up for taking that risk?"

The silence was total. Raig was glad. Glad she was taking his statement seriously. It mattered to him more than he'd ever imagined possible.

"I think so." She spoke clearly, her voice unhurried. "But I'm not sure, Rake, and I need to be. Oh, not about the nipping and biting bit. I'll give as good as I get. But forever? After only knowing you for a few hours?" She shook her head.

Not in negation, he thought, *more in bemusement.* He understood how she felt. He *didn't* understand this connection between them himself. He just knew it was there.

"Get real," Vairi continued. "What happened to try before you buy?"

"In this economic climate? Not a snowball in hell's chance. It's all cash on delivery these days. Or rather, no sale and return. That's the price we pay. If you want us, we're here for the taking. If not?" He shrugged. There was nothing else he could say.

With such an expressive face, her thoughts and doubts were easily read. He was ready to bet she'd now come out with a flat 'no', and he'd be driving her home and not driving *into* her. Wisely, he kept quiet, knowing it had to be her decision. He'd been taken aback by how easily he'd realized she was the one needed to make his life complete. As a kid, Raig had laughed at his da when he had told him that one look at his ma and he'd known she was the one for him—the shoe was now on the other foot. The photograph he had seen had whetted his appetite but not prepared him for meeting Vairi in the flesh. With the first look, he'd been smitten. He could have beaten his chest, Tarzan-style, jumping up and down, shouting 'mine'.

Vairi's shoulders straightened, almost because now her decision was made, it was time to impart it.

His cock shriveled as if it needed to hide—just in case. For fuck's sake, in case of what? *Get a grip. Hell, I'm acting like a wuss. Man up and face the music. Or whatever.*

Raig held his breath as he waited anxiously for her to speak and decide their fate. How on earth he would handle it if she came out with a flat 'no', he didn't want to imagine. Conversely, if they made love, and she said 'thanks but no thanks', would that not be worse? *Bloody hellfire*, he admonished himself angrily. *Stop second-guessing the woman and let her speak. And expand your vocabulary, why don't you? 'For fuck's sake' and 'bloody hellfire' are well overused.*

"Have you done muttering?" Vairi inquired as she sat down next to him. As he nodded with a wry grin, she smiled at him, her face lighting up. "I'm as worried as you are. It's not a one-way street, you know? You looked like a toddler who's been told he can't have a third lollipop. Man up."

He guessed what she was going to tell him would make him feel he wasn't getting a fourth. Even so, his cock reacted predictably to her smile. She noticed, of course. It would be difficult not to when his jeans now seemed two sizes too small.

"Down, boy. You haven't heard what I'm going to say yet."

Ah, did he really want to?

Chapter Two

He just knew she was about to cut out his heart. He could tell by looking at her now-unhappy face, her features pinched and drawn with no sign of that recent smile, just how she was affected and troubled by her soon-to-be-given answer.

Ah, bollocks.

Vairi took a deep breath and laced her fingers together in her lap. "Raig, I can't. I'm so, so sorry. I want you. Hell, do I want you. My body is throbbing thinking how bloody good I imagine we could — no, fuck it — *would* be together."

It was obvious to him just how she struggled to explain the way she felt. He shrugged. "Your decision, love." Even to himself he sounded a pompous git. Raig winced. It wasn't like him to behave that way. Mind you, he'd not been turned down before either. Unless one counted Eileen Craven behind the bike sheds in a 'you show me yours and I'll show you mine' session, aged fifteen and fourteen respectively.

Vairi's eyes sparked. "Exactly, and get the stick out of your arse and listen properly. Sheesh, it would be oh-so-easy to say, 'hey, yeah, why not'. Let you into my knickers and fuck. But forever? I can't promise that. Shit, all I know about you is what you've told me tonight, which is basically nothing. I've been stung once. I'm not going down that road again. The price is too high."

As he answered her in a bitter voice, he felt sick. "It's usually the bloke after the one-night stand, not the woman. Trust us to be doing it the other way round. I can't change the price, Vairi My Queen. I'd be doing us both a disservice.

It would be Cava, not Champagne, cheap and…" His voice trailed off as he shrugged once more. "Ah well, your decision. One I'll not be happy with, but one I'll respect. When you feel up to it, I'll take you home. Unfortunately, on a bike. Can you cope? Will you be needing a sick bag?"

He watched her face, recognized the regret and the determination there.

"I'll be fine. I'm more sorry than you will ever know, Raig. Hard though it is to believe, it's my world I've ripped apart as well as yours. For some unknown reason, I've fallen for you and fallen hard. Something I would have said was only in fairy tales and a load of crap in real life, but there it is. No, wait"—he had been about to butt in—"I have to be able to live with my conscience. I won't lie or bullshit about something so important. Yes, I want you and could easily say, 'hey, let's do it', then afterward tell you I'd changed my mind. But that would be dishonest and go against my principles, so I won't do that. Even if it means I go home hot, horny and irritable and rue the day I threw my bullet into the bin. It's too soon and too fast to make a decision like that." She sighed. "I'm ready to go if you are."

"Oh yeah, I'm ready. Not that it'll do me any fucking good." Shit, he really did sound like a whinging five-year-old who couldn't have the toy he wanted.

"Well, tough." Vairi stood over him and poked him on the shoulder. "You might be every woman's clit-rubbing dream, Rake, but you're a bloody sulky one." She stopped as she realized what she had said. The look of astonishment on her face would have been comical if he wasn't so bloody grouchy.

"Oh lordy, I said that out loud, didn't I?"

Raig nodded, and knew by the way she rolled her eyes his expression was still petulant. For Christ's sake, she'd admitted she could get off just thinking about him and still wasn't going to admit it was more than a passing fancy. His despair overwhelmed him—he'd run out of ideas. He saw the moment she lost the plot.

"Oh, for goodness sake, *grow up!* Sorry if I've thrown your life plans out of kilter, but that *is* life. Nothing ever goes as you expect it to. Build a bridge, man. Get over it. Shit, be thankful I'm being honest with you." She scowled and paced to the door. "Oh, don't bother to take me home. I'll get a taxi."

That annoyed him. "You most certainly will not. I'll get the helmets." He prayed that later she would remember his tone. He cared. Even if he seemed surly, he cared. In silence she waited by the door, one sparkly shod foot tapping ominously while he collected two bike helmets.

Still in silence, Raig escorted her out of the trailer, locked the door behind them and walked across the grass to a secure compound where he retrieved one of his pride and joys. Big, black and phallic, his motorbike was something he truly treasured. The throbbing power between his legs, the wind rushing past, the noise of wheels on Tarmac, arcing around corners, speeding down the straights, was truly sexual. It was even better with a willing woman riding behind, her pussy hard up to his ass, her arms tight around him, hands creeping into his crotch to brush his cock. To know when the bike ride was over, the body ride would begin.

He was on plums this time. His face stony and his cock hard, Raig wheeled the BMW toward her and settled on it.

"Helmet." He put his on and waited for her to comply. "Do you need help to get on?" God, he hated his tone, but hadn't the foggiest idea how to change it. He hurt. She'd hurt him and now…well, now he needed time to heal. If he could.

"Spitting the dummy out, Raig?" she inquired pleasantly as she swung her leg over the saddle and put a good three inches between her crotch and his butt. "Having a hissy fit because life doesn't revolve around you and your wants?"

Raig reached behind himself, catching her unawares as he pulled her snug against him. "I'm not the bad man here, Vairi. You won't catch anything by holding on to me." He didn't wait for an answer before he revved the engine and set off. If she chose to hang on to the grip bars instead it was no skin off his nose. "I'm trying not to be a pain in the ass. It's not bloody easy."

And if he believed any of that he'd also believe leprechauns were hiding in his trailer and messing up the wardrobe.

Vairi put her arms around him and held on to his waist as they rode in silence. She didn't ask how he knew where he was going, and he didn't offer the information. She probably registered the fact that Denny and Lorna must have told him. Unerringly, he drove to her cottage and pulled up by the gate. She unwrapped her arms from him as if he were poison. Raig left the engine idling, not bothering to see if she could get off unaided. If his touch was so undesirable, then sod her. He knew when he wasn't wanted.

"Lost your manners as well as your tongue?" Vairi spoke acerbically. "Well, Raig, you deserve it. Stop being a wanker." She took off the helmet and shook her head to lift her flattened hair. "Talk about having a tantrum because, oh dear, how sad, your plans have been thwarted. I bet you're not used to not getting your own way. Well, hello. Welcome to the real world, Padraig Whoever-you-are O'Shea. Give and take, not take and take. I might fancy the pants off you, you do things to my clit no one else ever has, even when you're speaking in that arsy voice. But think on, you're thirty-one and I'm forty-four. You're a roamer, I need to be here. You want happy-ever-after forever. I don't believe in either. Not a lot in common, then."

He didn't answer or try to justify himself. Everything she said was true, and he was ashamed of his behavior. If the truth be told, he was scared he would start blubbering like a baby as he listened to her ripping their lives to shreds.

"Oh, what's the use?" Vairi flung her hands in the air.

Raig had seen that done in films but never in real life. He'd always reckoned it looked over the top, but not now. It encapsulated everything he reckoned she thought about him. None of it positive.

"Bugger it," she said in a strange voice. "I'll go find my vibrator — luckily that didn't go in the bin with the bullet — then try to get drunk. Thank you for the lift home."

He found himself holding a helmet as she thrust it none too gently at his stomach and stalked away without waiting to see if he was going to answer her. He wasn't.

Instead he waited until she entered the house and slammed the door behind her so vehemently he jolted, pleased there was no part of his anatomy in the way. Especially the part that was standing up again and begging for immediate attention. Contrary or not. *Am I about to get my rocks off on her anger now? And that, Raig, my lad, is all up to you. Pitiful.* Sadly, though, he was going to have to do something about it. He couldn't function with a hard-on strong enough to break rocks. Definitely 'up'. Hands or no hands — that was the question. Women had a choice, hands or toys. Seemed like she would use both and have a drink. Damn if he wouldn't do the same, but without the toys. Unless he played solitaire as he jerked himself off.

Raig, you are *a jerk.* He used extreme care as he drove away, knowing his emotions were high. He suspected that perhaps driving such a powerful machine with his mind in turmoil was not a good idea. He had almost reached the fairground when he made his decision. He slowed the bike, turned and sped back the way he had come.

The stupid woman had left her key in the door. *Face it, it's my sodding fault. I made her so mad. She's probably half cut and rolling by now, drunk and wasted. All down to me and my piss-poor attitude.*

From inside the house he could hear voices, more than likely the TV. *Anyone could march in and surprise her*, he thought, as he did just that and made sure he retrieved the key and locked the door behind him. He didn't want them disturbed by anyone.

The voices turned out to be the TV, just as he'd suspected. As he looked from the hallway through the open lounge door, he could see Vairi sitting on the sofa, glass in hand, alternating between muttering words which sounded suspiciously like 'wanker', 'arsehole' and 'macho male prick', and singing off-key as she seemed mesmerized by the action on the set. He fixed the voices as those belonging to the couple on the screen. Now…what the —

Moving forward to stand behind the sofa, he put his hand on her shoulder. "Vairi McQueen, is that porn you're watching?"

The shriek as she spun around, splashing wine all over herself and the sofa, dislodging a bra from its place on the back of the couch to land at his feet, was loud enough to waken the dead. He wondered if his hearing would ever be the same again.

"Why is there a naked woman climbing out of a birthday cake on the TV?" he asked, interested.

"What? Oh, *Red Shoe Diaries* with David Duchovny. I used to lust after him. The best thing since sliced bread before you… Hold on." Scrambling off the sofa, she thumped him so hard on the chest he rocked on his heels. "You bastard. What the fuck am I doing discussing porn with you when you've just scared me out of my wits? You fucker, what the hell are you doing to me? How *dare* you barge in and frighten the life out of me?" The fear and anger in her voice were real and loud. "You left. Buggered off. Didn't want what I offered. No one-night stands for the moralistic high and mighty Padraig O'Shea, eh? So why are you here? Come to gloat?"

Something of his anguish must have shown, because as he stood there in front of her — clothes rumpled, no doubt with his face drawn and eyes tired, her door key held silently out toward her — he saw the anger drain from her face.

"Why, Raig?" she asked quietly. "I haven't changed my mind."

"I have. I lied," he said bluntly. "I'll take you however I can get you. An hour, a night. So be it. I'll take what you want to give." He paused and looked at her somberly. He was sure he must have shadows under his eyes, probably looked like something the cat had dragged in, and wondered if she still wanted him as much as he wanted her, with him looking as wrecked as he was.

"I'll tell you now though, Vairi My Queen, and I'll keep mentioning it over and over. I won't ever stop trying to change your mind about us," Raig said honestly. "Every hour, every day, I'll be chip-chipping at your defenses. Wearing you down. I'll keep on asking, Vairi, be mine. Be mine forever. One day you'll say yes to me. Then we will be one."

She squinted up at him and shook her head slightly as if she was trying to clear it. "Hell, you look like a romantic novel's cover. And ta-talk like the buck...no, back." She beamed. "All master... Full, a-a gor-gorgeous bod. Hold on. Why is there two Rakes? 'Swons enough."

Raig looked at her closely. Smashed. Just like that, from one sentence to another. Her glazed eyes were half closed, the overlarge wineglass she held at a dangerous angle almost empty. She smiled and looked at him owlishly, as if he held the answers to the meaning of life. He wished he did — he would do anything for her, he realized. She was the meaning of his life. This was where he should be. Forever. If that was not available, then shit, he would just take for now. Even if that included her smiling, smashed and — *oh hell* — nuzzling his neck as she fumbled with the buttons of his shirt, all while holding on to her glass, which was still tilted so the remains of the wine slopped perilously near to the rim.

"Ah, Vairi My Queen, we are both so foolish, are we not?" He tried to pry the wineglass from her hand, but she was having none of it.

"Shmine." She shook her head, groaned but still held on to the goblet with a grip that would do a wrestler proud. "You c'n get one tho'. In cu-cu'bud." Ah, his queen was well away.

"Come on, my love, let's share that one." He smiled cajolingly. However, like a true drunk, it was her glass, and no way was she going to share.

"No, get y'r own." She squinted. "Hey, you're him. Rake. Rake, who don't wanna make." She hiccupped and laughed. "An...an...lurv...sh. You dun' wan' me..." She ended on a wail. Then she took another hefty mouthful of wine and looked — as best she could — at her glass. "'S empty." She mourned. "Wh-where's bottle?"

He managed to keep his face straight. Just. *Oh, what a sore head she has set herself up for.* "Ah, all gone, my love. Shall we be getting you into bed now?"

"Mm, now thesh 'n offer." She handed him her glass and tugged his head down and planted a wet kiss on his face, moved her other hand to grab his butt and squeeze. "S'long as you comin'." She giggled. He had no idea what she was trying to say, as she stood in front of him, her luscious breasts, unfettered by a bra, pressed close to him. "Cos I c-come 'swell. Wanna, wanna see you c-come," she finished triumphantly, pulling on his hand as she swayed, and suddenly let go and fell back onto the settee. Behind her, on the TV, the woman wearing a pair of high heels and little else was still prancing around a cardboard cake. At any other time, his eyes would have been transfixed by what was on the screen. Now they were riveted on Vairi, trying to judge what she was going to do next. Nothing expected, that was for sure. She was smiling at him dreamily, holding her arms up to him.

"Gonna take me, Rake? Mmmm. I s'wanna feel yo' nated body 'n you nin'me."

Er, what?

Well, if she'd said what he thought she'd said, he'd promise that all right. But not now, when he could be anyone to her, not when she was so vulnerable. There would be no 'I didn't know what I was doing' the first time they made love. Or any other time.

"Come on, Vairi My Queen." He lifted her up from the sofa and she snuggled into him.

"S'nice, Rake. You nice. Le's go ta bed."

He kissed her cheek and winced as one flailing arm slipped between them and caught him a glancing blow, just missing his balls. Almost ouch. "Vairi, be bringing your hand up and hold on to me now, there's a love. Yeah, just like that." She pulled herself up and put her arms around his neck. "Not too tight now, or I'll be throttled, and we'll be on the floor. We'll be so much better on the bed. Loosen it now. There, that's my love. So which way?"

There was no answer. He looked down at the limp woman he was holding. She was out of it. No help there then. He carried her up the stairs and started to explore. On the third try, after a cupboard and a room that seemed to be used as a study, he found what he was looking for.

He glanced around with appreciation, taking in the downright sexy decor. He managed to pull back the cream silk cover on the bed and put Vairi down on the deep red sheet. Nice.

One eye opened. "Whaa?"

He waited, wondering if that was it. Would she lie there unmoving for the next umpteen hours? A twitch of his cock showed that part of him hoped not. *Behave. Taking advantage of women under the influence is not allowed.* When they made love, Raig intended they both knew exactly what happened and when. He said nothing as she closed her eye again briefly, as if in pain, before suddenly opening them both wide.

"Loo. Sheesh. Ah, please?" Vairi was trying to sit up.

"Ah, love, are you feeling sick?"

She put her hand over her mouth and moaned.

Raig gently helped her to her feet. "Where?" He had no bloody idea where the bathroom was. He'd not discovered it on his short hunt for the bedroom. Luckily, Vairi pointed to a door across the room.

"That way. Thanks."

He put his arm around her waist to guide her. "Am I needing to get a bucket?"

Vairi stopped dead and looked up at him. With, he noted,

remarkably clear eyes for one who had, he presumed, downed the better part of a bottle of wine so quickly. At least he imagined she had. He had no idea if the bottle has been full or not before she started drinking.

"Why would I need a bucket?" she asked in a puzzled voice. "I need a pee."

Oops. That was a close shave. "Then let's be getting you into the bathroom then." He opened the door and maneuvered her inside. "Can you, er…?" How the hell did he ask what he needed to know without sounding like a pervert?

To his amazement, Vairi laughed at him. "Yes, Rake, I can 'er'. I've been doing it by myself for a long while now. Thank you." She touched his cheek tenderly, then winced. "Shit, I've got a headache."

He bet she had. How come she'd been incoherent not five minutes before and now almost looked fresh as a daisy? Almost. He smiled his acknowledgment and went back into the bedroom, closing the door behind him. "Just shout if you need me."

Was that answer something along the lines of 'oh, I do'? Or was that wishful thinking? Whatever, he'd be practicing the limpet act for as long as he could. Well, until the real world intruded. Unfortunately, that time was drawing ever nearer. He heard the cistern flush and the noise of a tap being run. As the door opened, he turned, ready to take Vairi's arm and help her back to the bed. To sleep. Or so he told himself.

For someone seeming so inebriated a few minutes earlier, she was now looking fresh-faced and alert. *Definitely as fresh as a daisy.* Her face had a just-washed appearance, the tendrils of hair falling over her cheeks damp where they had been caught in the water. Without a scrap of makeup on, she seemed young and innocent. Raig would have sworn she was the one in her early thirties if he hadn't known better.

"How's the head?" he asked with caution.

"What?" She looked at him, curiosity in her eyes and tone of voice. "Oh, my head. Fine. Well, I've a bit of a headache, but all I've had to eat today is a slice of toast, two apples and a bag of crisps. No wonder I felt like shit." Her voice was upbeat. "Memo to self. Eat before you drink."

"Not feeling sick, or…?" He wasn't sure what to say. She appeared fine, didn't look drunk, however, not five minutes earlier she hadn't been able to stand upright, let alone speak coherently. He peered at her, saw how clear her eyes were, and swore. "Bloody hell, are you stone-cold sober already? After a bottle of wine in about an hour?"

She nodded sheepishly. "I don't get *drunk* drunk, only sort of drunk. Either I can't be bothered to drink, or I slur my words, feel awful, fall asleep for a few minutes and wake up with a headache. After an hour or so my headache goes, and that's it, over and done with. Tonight I'd decided I was going to try ever so hard to get rat-arsed, because I was so pissed off with you. You saw how far I'd got." She shrugged. "Although, to be honest, I don't think I want any more wine at the moment."

Raig stared at her until he saw her move uneasily. Her hands twitched and her face became rosy and flushed. *Good. Let her squirm.*

He lasted for all of five seconds before his anger got the better of him. For once he let rage overcome him and spill out. "You stupid bloody woman," he growled. "You didn't even lock the door. What if I was a rapist, or, or…?"

"An ax murderer?" she suggested helpfully. "The Phantom of the Opera? What's-his-name from *Psycho*? Good grief, men. And they say females overreact."

He could see her lips twitch. What was it with stroppy females? Didn't she *know* what a fright he'd had, finding the door unlocked and hearing voices? "Yes, or that. Anyone intent on something awful. Shit, Vairi, I was beside myself. Worried doesn't even begin to cover it." The humor of the situation began to sink in as he realized he was giving her hell, and she didn't have a clue why and found it funny.

Ha, I'll give her funny. "So, you're fine now? Not feeling sick, waving your wineglass, or wanting another bottle? In full possession of your wits, no memory lapse? Only a wee bit of a headache, is that it?"

Her expression wary, she nodded. "That's about it. Why?"

His smile was wicked, sinful. Slowly, his brogue strong, he spoke to her. "Oh, Vairi My Queen, I'll be showing you why. Take your blouse off."

"What?"

"Take...your...blouse...off. Nice and slow. Let me be savoring the view."

Vairi backed toward the door. He was there before her, enjoying himself now. She'd said she wanted him. Fine, she could have him. On his new terms. Try before you buy? No problem. She could try as many times as she liked, but on his conditions. Eventually she'd buy — he'd make sure of that.

"You wanted to 'try before you buy', my love." His tone was deceptively mild. Anyone who worked with him would know to be very wary. "It works both ways. Take your blouse off and let me see what I might be buying."

Head to one side, she considered his words. He could tell by the glint in her eyes, her rapid breathing as each exhale pushed her breasts out, that they excited her. By all that was holy, they excited him too. *She* excited him.

"Tit for tat, Rake. If I do, you do."

He'd won the battle, if not the war yet. "Why, of course, my love. I thought you'd never ask. See, I'm a gentleman, so I'll be following the old adage 'ladies before gentlemen'." He moved his hands to his shirt, opened it wide, attacked the clasp on his jeans and unsnapped it. Then he waited.

The determination he saw on her face as she mimicked his actions and went to open the top button of her blouse, while worrying her bottom lip with her pearly white teeth, would have normally stopped him in his tracks. But dammit, she'd hurt him, rejected everything he believed in — love at first sight, soul mates, *the* one. She'd rejected it all. He was human enough to crave revenge.

His stare followed her every move. Gradually first one then another button became separated from its fastening. Until she got to the fourth one, and her fingers slowed. Beneath them he could see the golden tan of her upper breast and the line where her skin paled. The beautiful, soft flesh that just showed. Raig's breath hitched. *Ah, be brave. Let me see all of you. Unless we make love in the dark, I'll be seeing you naked and next to me when humanly possible anyway.* He smiled. Encouraged her, willed her to continue.

Vairi inhaled. That essential button nearly popped as her breasts swelled. "Ready for this, Rake? To see me nude as I take my blouse off and let you see my breasts, my nipples puckered, waiting for you to touch them?"

Ah, sweet Lord, the words she spoke were so arousing. He moved uncomfortably, quelling the urge to rearrange the set of his cock. She noticed.

"Jeans a bit tight, are they, Rake?"

She taunted him but he understood there was no malice in it. Fun, sexy, sensual, arousing play.

"Ah, bless. It's not a case of 'do not adjust your set', you know. You can adjust any set, at any time." Vairi laughed and blushed. "I have *never* bantered sex talk in my life. God, have I been missing out." She spun around in a circle, her hands high above her head, and ended up facing him again. Her arms dropped to her sides and she bit her lip. "I like it. Do you?" She looked anxious again.

What a mass of contradictions, bless her. He loved it all. *Really love every last thing. And if that is weird, so be it.*

"Oh, do I ever. Minx," he said in an admiring tone. "My set is just fine, it's ready and waiting for the next act."

"O-kay." Vairi opened the next fastening. Raig held himself rigid as most of her luscious breasts appeared in his line of vision. She glanced at him, and what she saw in his still stance must have given her encouragement to continue. Her breasts spilled out, her nipples hard and, to his mind, begging for attention. He was hot, hard and aroused as she performed her — well, not a striptease, more a strip enjoy.

"Why, Vairi My Queen, maybe I should have been givin' you a hand." He couldn't help the brogue. It was always more pronounced when he was aroused, and boy was he that. "Beautiful. Will you be taking it right off now and letting me feast my eyes?" She colored, from embarrassment or arousal he couldn't tell. He hoped it was the latter, and that he could show his blatant admiration on his face. Then that in turn would give her the courage to take her arms from the sleeves and throw it on a nearby wicker chair.

"Your turn first. Take off your shirt."

Oh, so she is turning the tables, is she? No problem. With a smile that he was damn sure was all predatory male, Raig gripped the garment by each side and eased it over his shoulders. He dropped it onto the bed and watched her as she stared at him as his muscles rippled. Quickly, as if to do so before she lost her nerve, she shrugged out of her blouse. He could tell by the way she held each hand tight at her sides that she itched to cover her breasts but somehow refrained.

"Jeans," he said baldly. She didn't move, just swallowed convulsively. He lifted an eyebrow in question.

"I can't," she answered simply. "I'm scared." Her hands moved, but to his pleasure, not over her naked body. She stuffed them into her pockets instead and scuffed the floor with her toes.

He was incredulous, and a smile split his face. "Of me? Never. I would never harm a hair on the head of my future wife. Or anywhere else." He pseudo-leered, then grinned at the stupefied look on her face. "It's a determined man I am. It runs in the family."

She replied shakily. "Yes, well. As I can't see your future wife around, only me, I'm determined not to be a fool. Not to rush in, et cetera, et cetera, like I did before until I decided to put a stop to it. I'm not scared you'll hurt me physically, Raig." She rolled her eyes. "Sheesh, Denny would have your nuts in a vise if you did. No, it's more…oh, more *me*.

I'm scared of me." Then she did clasp her arms across her breasts in a defensive gesture as she tried to explain. The struggle to find the right words showed on her face and in her jerky movements.

Raig went and lifted her blouse from where it had landed and draped it around her shoulders in an oddly protective way. "There now, put it back on if you want to. We'll not do anything you aren't happy with." He felt like the biggest shit on earth. "Hell, Vairi, I want to keep you in my life, not scare you out of it. Now then, let's go and sit comfy. I'll make tea."

She gave him a watery smile but didn't put her blouse back on, leaving it as he had placed it. "No tea, Raig. Just sit and hold me and let me see if I can help you understand." He followed her to the bed and sat down on the edge beside her. She turned to him, and he watched as she tucked his hair behind his ears, tracing his diamond stud as she did. He took her hand, kissed the palm and curled her fingers over the spot.

"To keep my kiss safe," he told her.

Chapter Three

"Take a deep breath, and don't tell me anything you don't want to," he advised her as he held her hand and played with her fingers. "I'll wait for you as long as you want. Mind you, I'll be permanently horny and not be able to walk because of my hard-on, but hey." He shrugged dramatically, making her laugh.

"I don't think it'll be that bad," Vairi said softly. "I just got cold feet. I'm scared to trust anyone, especially a man. I worry that someone else is responsible for my happiness. I tried that once, and it damn near killed me when it all went wrong. If it hadn't been for Lorna, I don't know what I would have done."

"Lorna's dad?" he asked quietly.

She nodded. "I was twenty, a young twenty. He was thirty-five."

He winced inwardly. *Ouch.* No wonder she wasn't happy with their age gap.

She continued. "I fell hook, line and sinker. He was my lecturer at uni. Very charismatic, and he looked a bit like Don Johnson in *Miami Vice*. He knew all the strings to pull me in, and I let him. Then when I found out I was pregnant, he conveniently remembered the wife and two kids in his hometown. If it hadn't been for my mum and dad, goodness knows what I'd have done. They were great. They made sure I went back to uni after Lorna was born. I only needed to take one year out, and they helped me all the way. Even after I graduated, when she was little and when she started school, they were always there. I owe them so much." She sniffed. "Ah, it still makes me all teary when I think of it. They could have easily been pissy about it all. Gone on about my sense of right and wrong and bad choice of partner. But they didn't. They just gave me and Lorna all the love and encouragement we needed."

Raig cuddled her close. Her breasts brushed against his naked chest and sent frissons of excitement through him. He felt a rush of love for his brave lady. "Are they still alive, your mum and dad?"

Vairi laughed, her mood already lightening. "Are they ever. In their late sixties and touring Australia in a camper van. I keep getting e-mails saying 'guess what we did yesterday', complete with photos. Very unnerving, I can tell you. Yesterday's offering showed Mum doing a skydive. Last week it was Dad doing a bungee jump." She shuddered then giggled. "I certainly don't get my motion sickness from either of them. Mum insists she's going to learn to fly a microlight. Good on her, as long as she doesn't involve me."

Raig gave her another hug and said nothing as he simply enjoyed their closeness. This was what he wanted, now and forever. Inwardly he laughed at his fancifulness. Outwardly, he just smiled. "They sound great. Loving and loved."

He wondered if she knew just how sensual she looked. Her head resting on his shoulder, those gorgeous curls spread over him, her soft, pale breasts contrasting with his deeply tanned chest. His hands were itching to touch. His cock was not far behind in the wanting stakes. It stirred as they sat there, not speaking, just enjoying the moment.

"Raig, you're vibrating."

"Huh?"

"Vibrating," Vairi said again with a smirk. "And I don't think it's down to me."

"Ah, right." He'd been so immersed in his enjoyment of them together he hadn't noticed the sensations and vibrations coming from his pocket. "Shit." He moved one hand into the pocket and brought out his mobile. He looked at the number on the screen. "Trouble," he said briefly, before speaking into the phone. "Hello, Phil. What's up?" He listened, focusing on the voice at the other end of the line, and knew he was going to have to leave and return to the fair. "Okay, give me ten. I'll be with you as soon as poss. No, no, you had to. Fine, thanks." He hung up and turned to Vairi, who had been sitting quietly, still cuddled in, while he took the call.

"I'm sorry," he began regretfully, hoping he didn't sound as pissed off as he felt. "I need to go back. There's been a bit of a fight, and some thug tried to bottle Jonny. Otherwise, I'd be begging you to let me stay."

"Can I come?" She stood and began to finger the sides of her blouse.

"What?" He wasn't sure he'd heard properly.

"Can I come with you? I've decided it's about time I stopped not taking a chance in case it all goes pear-shaped. I'm forty-four years old, and if I can't cope with the vagaries of life by now, then too bad. If you'll give me two minutes to put my bra and blouse back on and grab my toothbrush, I'd like to go. If you want, that is…" She sounded very hesitant and unsure.

Raig was neither. "Bra, if you must, blouse, definitely. What it covers is for my eyes only. Toothbrush, I've got a new one you can have." He put his shirt on and fastened it. "And, my Vairi, I would love you to come back with me." He held his breath to hear her answer. As he was pulling his sweatshirt over his head, his voice was muffled, his face hidden, and it was impossible for him to see any clues in her expression regarding her reaction to his statement.

"Well, duh. Gah! I sound like a teenager. Right, two minutes." She got up, blouse flapping, and dashed out of the room into what she had called her dressing room. He heard drawers open and bang shut. In less than her self-allotted two minutes she was back with a tote bag over her shoulder, a clean blouse and jumper on, and if he was not mistaken, judging by the sensuous way her body was moving, no bra. "I even remembered knickers."

"Spoilsport."

"I didn't say I was going to wear them though, now did I? Right. I've just got to grab a jacket on the way out."

Raig watched, bemused as a happy, determined whirlwind sped past him, the hesitant, almost tearful woman of a few moments before gone as if she had never been. Would he ever understand women? *Probably not*, he thought. *Don't try, just go with the flow*. The flow, at that moment, was leading out of the bedroom and into the hallway.

He took hold of her and, swinging her into his arms then kissed her deeply and thoroughly and felt their tongues mesh and dance. His cock responded favorably as with a sensual little moan, Vairi rubbed against it.

It was with reluctance he moved back slightly. "Gotta go, Vairi My Queen. But I want you to promise me you'll ride with that beautiful pussy as hard up against my ass as possible. Something for me to hold on to as I sort out the aggression. Will you be doing that for us?"

"Try to stop me." He waited while she made sure the door was locked and followed her down the path, taking the chance to admire the sway of her butt as she walked. "Gorgeous ass." Her response was to give him the bird. He laughed.

This time the ride back was pure painful pleasure. At each turn of the wheel she leaned into him even more than he thought possible. The throbbing of the powerful engine intensified every emotion that bombarded him, and he fancied he could feel the heat from her, against his ass as they rode the machine together. Her arms were around his waist, her fingers as if by accident—and he didn't believe in those sort of accidents—brushing the rock-hard cock tucked inside his jeans, which demanded to be taken out and attended to. He'd make sure he got his own back later and tease her sexually—and unmercifully.

The ride was accomplished safely in minutes. There was very little traffic on the road. Unfortunately, it gave Raig plenty of time not only to worry about what he was going to find when he got back to the fair, but also to be extra aware of the way Vairi hugged him. Her scent in his nostrils make him wish he could turn the bike around and take her to bed. For hard and fast, soft and slow, long, lingering, mind-blowing sex. *No, not sex, lovemaking, never sex, not with Vairi, whatever she says to the contrary.* He brought the bike to a halt and focused on the immediate, not the hopeful, future.

"Here." He handed her a set of keys. "Green trailer, third from the end, cream blinds. I don't think you were in a fit state to take in your surroundings last time you visited it. Will you be okay?" he asked rapidly, his mind more on what he might find had happened. "Sure, no one will harm you, and if you get lost, ask anyone connected with the fair for directions."

"Well, duh, you go and be all boss-like and powerful. I'll be fine and see you whenever." She winked. "I'll be a-waiting."

Raig grinned. "I'll be as quick as I can, but make yourself at home." He gave her another hard, scorching kiss that she returned with enthusiasm.

"Don't worry about me, I'll be fine," Vairi assured him. "Let's hope everything else will be. You go and help Jonny." Another swift kiss, and he watched as she strode away, long legs eating up the distance, butt tight underneath her jeans. He sighed before turning toward the trailer they used as an office, laughingly called the Ready Room after *Star Trek*. Goodness knew what he was going to find there.

What he found were two policemen — luckily both known to him — Phil, the fair's manager and two surly lads of about nineteen glowering and swearing at all and sundry.

"Where's Jonny? Is he okay?" he asked urgently. He and Jonny were cousins, but more than that, had been best friends ever since the early days of their fairground traveling, watching each other's backs, egging each other on and taking the other's blame when necessary.

"Doc's checking him over, but he didn't seem too worried,"

the taller policeman said. "These two specimens of the youth of today thought they would have a go at him, because he politely asked them not to urinate where the world and his wife could see. And, I hasten to say, laughed at their tackle. According to one of the women they surprised, they were pitiful. She said she'd seen better on a dog. A Chihuahua." He snorted as he obviously struggled not to laugh. "She also said that was doing the dog a disservice. Her female companion likened one to a misshapen, wizened cornichon, and the other to a kid's crayon."

"Ah." Raig managed to keep his face straight as he relished the descriptions. "So what happens now?"

"We're waiting for the van, then it's off to the station for them. A fair number of charges— Shut up, you," he directed one of the youths, who began to swear again. "My, he's got a pitiful vocabulary. Do the youth of today not know there's more cuss words than fuck and shit?" The policeman shook his head. "Sad really, a vocabulary like his tackle, evidently."

Raig laughed and ignored the 'fuck you, you bastard' that the tallest—and scruffiest—lad uttered. A commotion outside the trailer announced the police van, which arrived at the same time as Jonny and the doctor.

"No concussion, but he'll have a sore head and some interesting bruises for a day or so," the doctor said easily. "I've put five stitches in that thick scalp of his. Oh, and he'll be sporting a couple of black eyes as well."

"Just as well he's no oil painting then." Raig tried to sound upbeat to hide his anger and dismay at the sight of his cousin but felt he wasn't succeeding. "No one will notice anything different."

"Cheers. Thanks, boss. Ever heard the expression 'it takes one to know one'?" Jonny smiled as best he could with a cut lip.

"Exactly." Raig made his voice deliberately smarmy. "That's how I'm knowing you're not one." His comments made them all laugh, with the exception of the youths, who started to sneer something derogatory before they were hustled out.

Silence reigned for a few seconds before one of the policemen cleared his throat. "So, we'll be needing statements from you and Phil, Jonny. Are you up to it now?"

Jonny nodded and flinched as he did so. "Let's get it over and done with. Raig, you go back to wherever...or whoever." He tried a wink, which ended in a grimace.

"I'll wait," Raig said briefly, resigned to another hour or so before he could rejoin Vairi. Shit, if she hadn't gotten fed up waiting and taken a taxi home, she'd probably be asleep when he finally returned to her side. He remembered the look she had given him when they'd parted and hoped with everything he had that neither scenario would be the one that played out.

It was over an hour later before he was finally able to walk through the dark and deserted fairground. The smells of diesel, chip fat, popcorn and candy floss hung faintly in the still air. The moon—three-quarters full—showed his path through the stalls and rides, helping him to avoid any obstacles. Beside him Jonny was moaning about the promise Raig had extracted from him not to work the following day. In the end Raig lost his temper.

"For fuck's sake, Joh." He used Jonny's childhood nickname on purpose. "Stop moaning. Yeah, life's a bitch. Tough shit. You're fucking lucky, do you know that? Those mean little fuckers could have had a knife. Then what? Dear Aunty Chrissie, sorry, but... Shit, I don't even know what hymns you want." The last was to try to lighten the atmosphere and stop himself from choking on a sob.

"All Things Bright and Beautiful."

"Eh?" What the hell was Jonny going on about?

"The hymn," Jonny said in an embarrassed tone. "And you can add that stop all the clocks stuff as well. I might as well hedge my bets over who gets me where. So, I want that bit from Ecclesiastes about to every time there is a purpose, with what's-her-name singing it."

"Judy Collins? Or The Byrds?" Why were they having this conversation?

"Her, moron. So Judy Collins. Flowers —"

"Enough." They reached Jonny's trailer. Raig turned to his cousin and took a deep breath. "All I'm saying is, for Christ's sake, take it easy. Please."

Jonny nodded, his battered face showing his thanks for the support. "Sure, and thanks."

"Okay. Well, ring me if you need me."

That elicited a crack of laughter. "I'm thinking you'll be needing her more than I'll need you." He nodded across the expanse of grass toward Raig's trailer, where lights showed welcomingly through the curtains. "Lights on, curtains drawn, a sappy smile. You don't need a degree to know you've a woman waiting."

It could have been much worse, Raig thought as he nodded to a security guard and continued to walk toward his home. It only took a couple of idiots fueled on booze, or worse, to start an incident that could easily escalate into something really nasty. He also suspected Jonny could be right. He wanted, *needed*, Vairi so much every part of him ached, not just the parts he intended to become intimately involved with her body very soon.

If she had fallen asleep, he would damn well wake her up, Raig decided as he reached the first of the trailers. His was the only one with lights still on. Even Jonny had decided shut-eye was needed. However, Raig knew there was no way would he be able to sleep without coming one way or another. His preferred way was deep inside her, as he experienced the sensations as she contracted around him and screamed his name. His cock throbbed unbearably just thinking about it. He could almost feel her wetness as he imagined putting his fingers inside her and making her writhe with pleasure. Those first few discoveries of what turned your partner on, then enjoying them together, were as important as the end result. As he had once heard one of the older students at uni say, '*To fuck with finesse and fact-*

finding is far superior and more satisfying than to fuck fast and furious'. Okay, the guy had thought he was a poet, a master of alliteration, and had often assailed his fellow students with his so-called words of wisdom, but on that occasion Raig felt he had expressed how he himself felt. Those first gentle discoveries were precious.

Another security guard passed. It was a sad necessity that safety measures needed to get tighter each year. When he was a kid, the only precautions taken had been the fairground staff themselves, plus an assortment of family pets. Now they had a dozen or so men employed purely for that purpose. Although they still had the same motley assortment of animals, including a couple of geese, fondly known as Samcam and Dave.

His pleasure surged as he approached the trailer, the lights through the closed blinds a beacon to welcome him home. Thank goodness Vairi hadn't left the slats open for anyone to look inside and wonder who she was. Those stories would circulate soon enough. He'd like some time with her without the fair monitoring their every move. Or anyone else.

As he climbed up the steps to the door, the faint sounds of music filtering out. Not loud enough to disturb passersby, it was just loud enough, it seemed, to beckon him, call to him. Sensible for once, she had locked the door. Raig knocked softly and wondered briefly what the hell he would do if she had fallen asleep and didn't hear. He needn't have worried. Within a few seconds the door swung open, and her lush, inviting mouth fixed on to his with a toe-tingling kiss. Her arms drew him inside, and a bare foot kicked the door closed behind him.

She wore his robe, the sleeves turned back several times, the tiny fiddly buttons on it undone, the belt around her waist twice, and hopefully nothing else. Up until that moment he'd hated that bathrobe, with to him, those stupid unnecessary buttons. He swore his mum had bought it for a joke to remind him that he should be a metrosexual male, not an out and out macho one. It hadn't worked and he'd shoved it to the back of his wardrobe. Ignored it. Now it was the nicest item of clothing he'd ever owned.

"Mmm, you can be greeting me like that, Vairi My Queen, anytime," he murmured as he moved the toweling material to one side, put his lips to her neck and nuzzled the silky soft skin there. "Let me be locking the door, and you can have your wicked way with me. Lead me astray, you older hussy you."

"Ha. Not so much of the older, please, or I might decide I can't satisfy a youngster like you and take myself home to my lonely cold bed."

"Lips sealed," Raig said and mimed a zip over his mouth.

"That apart, the rest will be my pleasure. Once you tell me how Jonny is. What happened?" She watched him with concern, *her* eyes wide and troubled as he checked the door and moved back to her.

Raig rolled *his* eyes. "Two of your fine town's non-finest decided they couldn't be bothered to find a toilet. When Jonny objected, they took *their* objections out on him. Five stitches in his scalp, split lip, broken tooth and a pounding head. To say nothing of the bruises. Some punters saw what was going on, got security and called the police. Phil, the fair's manager, was with them, saw what was happening and phoned me."

"Why phone you?" Ouch, he should have known she'd pick up on that one.

To stall, he leaned into the fridge and took out a bottle of wine. "Want one?"

She rested against the work surface. "Yes, please, and don't change the subject. Or say it's because you're best friends or cousins or something. 'Fess up."

He'd known this conversation had to take place sooner or later, but had hoped for later rather than sooner though. He poured two glasses of wine and gestured to the settee. "And while I'm remembering, I'll be telling you, how much I like you in that robe you've got on, especially as you've ignored the buttons and just belted it. It suits you much more than it suits me. The way it covers you makes me want to unwrap you and discover the jewels it hides. Bloody perfect. I'm drooling at the thought of what's waiting for me."

"That's the idea," she said with a faint blush as she sat close to him. "Tease and hint. That's as far as it goes until...?" She raised an eyebrow.

He got the hint. "Well, my love, it does that and more." He watched as she opened her mouth to speak, loving the play of emotions crossing her face and the sparring with exciting sexual undertones that was making him rock-hard. "Right, now I'll be telling you why Phil contacted me."

She nodded and took a sip of her wine. "Please."

Show and tell time. Raig took a deep breath. "Well now, yes, we are friends and cousins. His ma is my da's wee sister, but I suppose I should also make it clear that I'm not just his boss, the fair is mine. It was my da's, but he's well retired now and handed it over to me."

There was a silence before Vairi began to laugh. "So you're Mr. Big?"

"That depends on where you'll be looking, Vairi My Queen." Pure innuendo dripped from his voice. "Why are you saying that?"

She shook her head, something amusing her. "Oh, no reason, although I'm sure I heard somewhere you don't travel all the time. You're an investment banker or something?"

"Or something," he agreed drily, having no inclination to go any deeper into his professions—any of them. "Every year I take six weeks or so to travel, keep my eye in. Phil is my manager, immensely capable, but it gives us a chance to catch up, to sort out anything he feels unable to do by himself. Not that there is much of that. He's good, is Phil."

"I'm glad." Vairi had set down her wineglass. Now she turned to him and put her hands under his T-shirt. She unerringly found his nipples and alternately squeezed and soothed the hard nubs. It was amazing and, as ever, his cock immediately strained for attention. Raig moaned and swore his eyes crossed. "Ah, love…"

"Yes?" she continued. "You see, I have this problem I need your help with."

Oh fuck, so do I. "Ah, and what might that be?" To say he was enjoying himself was an understatement. Never before had his nipples seemed so responsive to a touch.

"I've a need for a man." She parodied his lilt. "Not just any man, one special man with an earring and hair to his shoulders. Can you be helping me?"

"Well now, I might just be the man for you. I've the hair and the earring. And a real talent for undoing tiny little buttons if you do them up?" He licked his lips and looked pointedly at the fastenings that usually annoyed him like crazy. Now the thought of undoing them on her and revealing her inch by inch was more than enticing. "Will I be the one?"

Vairi laughed softly, sending erotic shivers down his spine. "I'll be thinking you will. If you can be undoing the buttons. Give me a sec." She turned her back for a second or two then swung around to face him, the buttons now in their buttonholes "How's that? Can you help me?"

"Watch me," he said fervently. "There's one from the bottom." He made sure his hands were busy as he spoke. "And a kiss on the ankle to keep you interested. Now one from the top, oh see? Such a beautiful swell of the breast for me to nip and soothe." He did as he described. "Ah now, this is interesting. Do I still go one up then one down, or do I get greedy?" He considered, his head to one side as he toyed with various buttons, opening none. Vairi's breathing was uneven, her eyes half closed as she watched his actions. She raised one hand and caressed his neck as she left the other lying loosely by her side. Raig watched her clench it tight and slowly release her fingers as he ran a hand from her ankle to her knee.

"Oh, now, what else have we here?" He returned his attention to the next button to be opened at the bottom of robe. "Do you know," he queried conversationally as he nimbly continued opening the tiny clasps and ran erotic nips and kisses either along the line of her throat, the plump lushness of her breasts, or the fine skin of her ankle and calf. "I was thinking earlier, when I was in my strop, that I'd missed my chance to get into your knickers. Now as these buttons open, and more and more of your delectable body is revealed, I realize that soon I'll be getting my chance. Will I not?" He was perplexed as her body shook with laughter.

"Well," she sputtered. "I suppose you could, if I went and put some on."

Chapter Four

"Wha—" Sheesh, what did he sound like? His slipped his hand under the few buttons still fastened and moved unerringly upward to feel soft, silky skin, springy curls and a wet, beautiful clit. "Oh my, my Vairi, you truly continue to surprise me in the most magnificent ways. All this for me? What a welcome."

"Mmm," she sniggered, and reddened. "Well, I had a shower, and there didn't seem much point in putting clean underwear on when I was hoping you'd just take them off again."

"Indeed not." He eased his fingers inside her as he spoke and danced and scissored them together, moving them in then out to caress and tease her clit. "It would have used up precious time, time when I could be slipping my fingers inside you like I am now. So much more fulfilling, I'm thinking." With his other hand, he made short work of the rest of the buttons, smiled his appreciation as the two sides of the robe fell apart, revealing her body, tanned and toned with tantalizing white strips across her breasts and pussy, and sighed in reverence at what was revealed. "No nude sunbathing then, Vairi My Queen? As a possessive man, I like the thought that these precious places are not for everyone to view, just me."

Her eyes, which had been half closed, seeming with passion, sprang open. "No one possesses me, Padraig O'Shea. No one. I am my own person, not anyone else's. Understand?" Those deep blue eyes flashed at him, daring him to disagree.

He didn't. *Oh my. Feisty, as well as arousing. Be still my heart.*

"I wasn't meaning it like it sounded, Vairi," Raig said earnestly. "I would never dream of possessing you in that way. I just like the idea that you don't bare your all for all to see. I don't like the idea of other men seeing those glorious breasts and that secret, sensitive clit. I'm man enough to enjoy the idea that they are for my eyes only. That is my idea of possessive. I'm hoping you'll feel the same about me. I don't bare my all for others to see. Although," he said humorously, "I confess, I do go topless."

He saw her lips twitch. "You sod. There I was, getting my knickers in a twist—well, I would have been if I'd any on—and you disarm me, poof, just like that. How the hell do you do it?" She shook her head. "However, I can see you are daring enough to go topless, you shameless creature. No tan lines." She pulled his sweatshirt up as she spoke. Buttons popped as she swiftly sent his shirt the same way. Raig helped by removing his fingers from inside her as the top came over his head, only to replace them immediately after and caress her clit as he did so.

"Does that feel good, my Vairi?" *Needy or what?*

"Oh God, yes. Very good. Shit, Raig, you've got magic fingers." Vairi panted the words. "But I want you in me." She gasped. "Feel your cock in me." Her hands stole to the hard ridge pushing against his jeans, and circled it over the denim. "I want to see."

"Patience. We've all the time we want, there's no rush." He soothed with his voice as he excited her with his hands.

Vairi screamed. Raig swiftly covered her mouth with his, drank in her pleasure and held her tightly as she shook and came in an explosive climax.

"Hell," she gasped. "In me. Now. Please, now...aah." Raig flexed his fingers and felt her shudder again as her hands moved to his fly and she clumsily began to open the zip. He drew in his breath sharply. She seemed to understand why.

"Don't worry," she said reassuringly. "I won't catch you in it. I've a feeling your cock is much too important to both of us to do it any damage."

Her breath hitched as her fingers encountered his silky hardness. Raig was somewhat relieved she made sure they were a barrier between his flesh and the metal teeth of the zipper.

"I need to know what it's like to have you deep inside me, Rake, touching my soul." She laughed shakily. "Hell, fanciful or what? But oh-so-true." The concentration on her face as she struggled with his jeans excluded any other emotion.

Raig was moved by her statement. He couldn't find the words to describe his emotions so he kissed her breast as he kept up the pressure inside her and alternated between soothing and caressing. He could tell by the way she moved awkwardly to pull his jeans off he wasn't making it easy for her, but he thought by her choppy breathing and the indrawn breath as he touched her clit it was worth it. Especially when she started to play him at his own game and began to run her fingers up and down his already throbbing dick. Her feather-light touches equally excited and inflamed him and he was damn sure his cock was slick with pre-cum. He moaned—in pleasure or pain, he wasn't sure. Whichever, he knew it was the prelude to the explosive emotions of making love.

"Oh, love..." Her voice petered out. "Lovely." She spoke so quietly he strained to hear. He could have sworn she was going to use the 'L' word before she amended it. One day, he vowed to himself, she would say it. Out loud, to him, about him.

Vairi stilled her hands and her clever arousal stopped. He looked at her closely, saw the worried look, and decided to try teasing. "What's up? Other than me, thanks to those clever, dexterous hands of yours. I was so enjoying the way they were turning me on, then they stopped. You've gone away from me, my love. Where are you?"

She shook her head as if to clear it again. "I'm here. Sorry. Well, anyway...I, er..."

"Realized overwhelming love for me?" He thought she

would laugh. Instead she looked stunned.

"Lust," she replied emphatically.

Too much so? He could only hope it was a case of the lady protests too much.

"I am totally lusting after you, Rake O'Shea. Can you *please* breathe in and let me concentrate on not catching anything I shouldn't? Because once I get these damn jeans off your legs" — she smiled with sexual promise — "I'm going to taste you."

"Make me come? With your mouth?" His fingers moved again. "As I put my tongue into you, lick your pussy, suck your clit?" Had he gone too far with his frankness? Judging by the wicked smile, he thought not.

She slapped his legs lightly. "Let me concentrate, or there'll be no coming. Only going...to hospital."

"Ouch. I'll let you concentrate." Still, he touched her clit, even as he breathed in and felt the zip part, and his cock pushed above tight black briefs, making its presence known. As he'd thought, his pre-cum glistened over its length. He hoped it made her itch to taste it as much as he wanted to taste her. "Taste then. As far as I know, it's not illegal. Ah, Vairi, I so would be loving to feel you do that."

She said something, too low for him to hear.

"Darlin'. Why the mutters? Is there something wrong?" He wasn't sure if he was goading or inquiring. "Are you wanting me to stop playing with your clit? Move my hands away?" He suited his actions to his words when she halted him by pushing his fingers more firmly into her then moaned softly.

"Do not *dare*, unless you think I'm not capable enough to get you out of those jeans and into my mouth while I'm writhing in ecstasy." Her smile was a challenge. One he picked up and took immediately as he flexed his fingers and began to pluck, nip, soothe and caress.

Vairi arched her back as if a charge of electricity shot through her. "Damn it, Rake, I'm going to come before I even get your bloody jeans off. Stop it." With shaky hands she swatted his leg. "Lift your butt so I can get them down."

He complied rapidly, but even so he made damn sure he never stopped those sensual movements with his fingers. She seemed to have difficulty in getting the butter-soft denim down his legs and over his feet. Raig had already kicked off his shoes in order to facilitate her actions — his practice of not wearing socks whenever possible was a definite bonus.

He sensed her eyes on him as she checked out his body and, he thought optimistically, feasted on what she could see. Raig gave himself a mental check over. His legs were tanned up to a line across his upper thigh, then the white skin extended to just below his waist. His torso was tanned, his face and arms ditto. He waited in anticipation for her next move.

She ran a finger up his leg and smiled provocatively at his indrawn breath, and held her finger tantalizingly near his cock, which of course twitched in encouragement. A throaty laugh showed she was aware of the effect she had on him.

"Hot holidays?" Her finger traced the defining line along his thigh between tan and no tan before slowly moving upward again.

He nodded and swallowed to try to get enough saliva to speak. "Working here mainly. I'm too busy to do much else. Although it makes you tan, clothes are annoying. It's hot and sweaty and thirsty and —"

"Yes, well, I get the gist," she interjected in haste, her skin flushed, the pulse at the base of her throat fast. He saw the brief glance she gave his erection, now so hard as to almost shout for attention. Didn't she comprehend it was her who was having the effect on him? His cock begged — cried — to go inside her and come there. It seemed she thought the same way.

"Raig, I need you. I want to experience you filling me, pleasuring me. Please?"

Thank God. If only he could hold off long enough to make

it more than a 'three thrusts and it's over' encounter. *Right then...*

"Well, Vairi My Queen, your wish is so very truly my command. But I'll be needing to be moving for a second." Slowly, eroticism in every deliberate motion, he slipped his fingers out of her with a last sensual touch on her clit before he stood up unhurriedly and pulled her with him. "I was thinking the bed would be more comfortable maybe, and I need to be getting condoms."

He watched her blush all the way to her hairline. Was she worried about his bluntness? He wouldn't have thought so. Surely she would be happy to know he practiced safe sex?

"Oh fuck." She groaned. "I cannot believe I'd forgotten about the importance of those little bits of latex. Shit, my cousin even works for a condom company! It shows how long it is since I got down and dirty with any... Oh fuck again. Sorry. My big mouth."

He had to laugh at her embarrassment as he led her into the small, well-appointed bedroom where most of the space was occupied by a king-size bed covered by a navy blue duvet. When he'd had the option, Raig had gone for bed space rather than walk-around space. He opened a drawer in the cabinet above the bedhead and exhaled in relief.

"Phew. I was wondering if there were any in here. I don't often have a need for them." He saw and interpreted her interrogating glance correctly. "I don't go in for casual sex, love. Contrary to what it may look like, I'm very choosy. But I do keep a stash for any of the lads who might need one and haven't got any. As does Phil. The last thing we want is paternity claims left, right and center. I'll tell you now, I'm damn glad I stocked up recently." He put a handful of silver foil packets on top of the cabinet.

Vairi laughed and lifted her tote bag off the chair where he noticed she'd left it earlier and opened it. Slowly she put her hand inside and withdrew a box of condoms, putting it on the other tiny bedside cabinet.

Bloody hell. In the heat of the moment, he had all but

forgotten about that important little package, and she'd been the sensible one.

"I was a Girl Guide, so I'm always prepared." She turned, and rubbed her hands up and down his chest, lingering on each muscle in turn. "Oh, Rake, I love touching you, seeing how I affect you." She ran her hands across his nipples and pinched each nub hard enough to sting. As he took a sharp breath at the explosion of sensation, she laughed softly. The feeling of her hands on his skin and hair was combustible, and it was he who was going to combust. It was so bloody hard to let her set the pace, let her discover what she wanted and how she wanted it.

"Oh hell, Raig." She was muttering under her breath so quietly he had to strain to hear. "I couldn't tell you the last time I felt like this. What is it the mags say, 'Unleash your sexuality'? Well, mine's about to be unleashed big time. I hope you don't mind."

Very slowly, she moved her hands lower down his body as she spoke, and to his delight she trailed her lips slowly after them. Each touch left a slash of heat that burned into him and increased his arousal.

"I'm sipping and savoring you, my Rake. Every inch, all the way."

He watched as a look of devilment spread across Vairi's face.

"Ooh, Raig, you're so stiff." She paused. "All over. Relax why don't you." Her mouth reached his balls and she gently rolled them around with her tongue and fingers, alternating touching them and his cock.

He nigh on hit the roof as he saw stars. Was he cross-eyed? It wouldn't surprise him one bit. "Relax? Jeez, Vairi, there's no bloody chance of that. You're going to make me come before I get anywhere near inside you if you keep doing that. It's fucking amazing. Aahh! So a-maz-ing." The insistent pressure of her mouth had him at his boiling point. "God almighty, woman, I might never recover."

"Can you feel yourself? You're swelling and pulsing in

my mouth. Making me wet and ready for you." She cocked her head to one side without releasing him. "Ah, decisions, decisions. Do I carry on and make you come in my mouth? Or am I selfish and ask you to come deep inside me? Or both?"

"Oh, definitely both, my love." Was that croaky voice really his? "I'm sure we will have the stamina. It's over to you. I'm happy to see how you decide." He put his hands on her shoulders to steady himself and they tightened as she pulled him farther into her mouth.

"Jeez, it's been a long time since I've felt a cock in my mouth or anywhere. Oh shit, shit, *shit!* That is so un-PC. Gah, I'm sorry."

He could tell she was mortified by the way her mouth stopped moving and she dipped her head. Instead of agreeing that 'yes, not good to talk about past conquests', he laughed. "Ditto re me in a mouth or pussy," he reassured her. "But I'm sure it's like riding a bike. Once you're back on again, you'll remember everything you need to know."

"Well." She gurgled. "Here's hoping. And that I remember how to overcome my gagging reflex. Now, let me see." She adjusted her head and drew him even deeper.

Raig groaned. "Hell, Vairi, I'm going to come inside your mouth and shoot down your throat if you carry on." He held on to his sanity and his cum by a thread. Every single fiber in his body was taut and ready to break. However, he was damned if he was going to let it happen until he was good and ready.

Slowly she moved her mouth up almost to the tip, giving herself the chance to speak throatily in between moves. "That's the idea. I'm going to make you scream for me, Raig. I'll milk you, drink you and love you." He reckoned she began to take him inside her mouth again before she truly understood just what she had said.

He noticed however. Like a wise man, he kept his mouth shut. His pleasure was too high to even begin to think how she meant '*love*'. *But I know*, he thought on a spike of ecstasy as she drew him deep into her throat, and his cock responded in anticipation of all to come by throbbing at the brink of pain. *I know it has to be more than sex. These feelings she's giving me, the intensity, the amount of Vairi I'm getting. It's love, even if it is love given unknowingly.* The soft sweep of her tongue as it caressed the hard length of him, her mouth as it sucked him deeper made him writhe in ecstasy. Her teeth nipped gently before her lips soothed. It was, he deduced hazily, fucking marvelous in any sense of the word. Perhaps when he had breath to spare, he'd tell her. If, he surmised as sensations overwhelmed him, he ever did.

Raig registered the fact that his legs were trembling. Sheer willpower kept him upright instead of collapsing onto the bed. Vairi worked her mouth cleverly, as she brought him ever closer to climax. One thought was going over and over through his mind. That he was either going to have to beg her to stop or come deep inside her, filling her mouth and her throat with his cum.

With a mischievous upward slant of her face, which gave him a whole new set of sensations to contend with, she smiled provocatively before taking him as deep down her throat as possible and milking him. He had no options left to him. Raig came hard and fast, his breath choppy, his pulse racing as he shouted, shuddered and spilled into her mouth. He clutched her shoulders as she sucked and swallowed every last drop of semen, his whole body shaking with the intense emotions rolling over him in waves. His knees were giving way, but she still held him captive in her mouth until finally, as his last shudder of passion subsided, she slowly stroked her mouth up his still-hard length, pressing teasing kisses as she moved her lips away with — it seemed — regret.

A gentle push on his abdomen had him fall back onto the bed, with his legs and feet dangling over the edge. He was too spent to move them. Too spent to talk. He looked at her still kneeling next to the bed, tiny drops of his cum on her lips, a satisfied smile on her face. When he got the energy, that smile of satisfaction was going to be for a whole different reason. A pity that he was so drained, as he was damn certain he had no idea when that energy would be in him.

Raig patted the bed next to him. "Oh, love, I've not the words to describe how honored I'm feeling." He knew the brogue was there, hoped she'd understand it was due to passion and not put on. When in the throes of deep emotion, his accent was strong but he couldn't help it. "If you'll be giving me a week or two to recover, I'll be repaying the compliment. For now, can I just be giving you a cuddle?"

With a chuckle she stood, went into the bathroom and returned with a damp cloth in her hand before moving to lie on the bed, her head on a pillow.

"Come on, get the energy to lie down properly." She shook her head pseudo-mockingly. "I don't know, youngsters of today, no stamina or staying power." She was openly laughing as he slowly dragged himself up the bed to lie at her side. He was glad she couldn't read his mind. Oh ho, was she ever in for a shock.

He got the shock first. Waiting until he was settled beside her, Vairi used the cloth to lovingly, or so it seemed to him, wipe his semi-erect penis. It responded as best it could, better than he could have predicted. While the spirit was very definitely willing, the flesh might need a bit longer. Not that much longer though, he'd bet. Raig rolled to his side, firmly removing her hand and the rag.

"No more. I'm preserving all my energy to show you just what we youngsters are capable of. I hope you're not one of these people who need their eight hours, love, because I'll need to be up in less than six hours, and I'm not talking about my cock here, that's going to be up much sooner. I'm saying you'll not even be getting those six hours to sleep. Count on it."

"Oh, I will," she said with a purr. "And you know? I'm looking forward to every minute of not sleeping." She traced the tattoo of a bluebird on his left shoulder. "Why this?"

Lord, now, how to answer that and not drop himself or his alter ego in the shit? With as much honesty as possible.

"A friend's sister who died loved them. My friend said it was the bird for hope. No, not a girlfriend, just a girl who needed a friend." And he'd failed her sister. His first job as an undercover investigative reporter and Maya had been battered and bruised by her abuser before his team had unearthed enough evidence to take to the police. Rita, his friend, had gotten married, had a son, and now lived in Australia, but Raig still felt, deep down, he should have moved faster to help, even though he knew it had been impossible. It had taken a long while for him to accept he couldn't necessarily do everything he wanted as he wanted, but even so… Raig wrenched his mind away from the past.

"Ah well, I'll be making it worth your while to be awake." He moved suddenly and pinned her arms above her head, her robe still on her shoulders, bunched underneath her as she lay on her back and looked up at him. "You can hunt for the other tattoos later." Raig could see both interest and desire in her eyes. *Well*, he vowed as he stared back at her, *soon there will be passion showing there also*. With his spare hand, he rummaged in his cabinet drawer. Finding what he wanted, he held it up and showed it to Vairi. "Will this be moving too fast for you, Vairi My Queen?"

Vairi shook her head. "Oh, I don't think so. I'll have a safe word?"

He nodded. "Of course. Although I can promise there will be no need to use it." He watched the expression on her face as she considered his words.

"Regardless, we'll have one."

"Sensible."

"Oh that's me. Sometimes." She paused. "Rum." His face must have mirrored his thoughts regarding the vagaries of a woman's mind, because she laughed. "I really do not like rum. Not even in a punch or Singapore Sling. Tastes like cough medicine. The only time I was almost properly not able to snap out of it drunk was on rum. Er, what are you going to do?" She didn't sound scared, just curious.

"Nothing you don't want, I promise you. Are you okay with that?"

"Well," she said reasonably, "as I don't know what is what, I don't know if I'm happy with it or not. But I trust you. Denny and Lorna do." She shut her eyes briefly, and when she opened them again he saw her determination and, he thought, excitement there. "I'm ready to take that leap into the dark with you."

Never were words more erotic.

"Will you close your eyes for me?"

"Literally in the dark then?" She smiled and closed them. He expelled the breath he hadn't realized he was holding.

"Trust, Rake. I trust." He noticed she was using the nickname she'd bestowed on him. It made this moment more special, he decided. More intimate.

"I won't break your trust." He moved off the bed, kissing her lips softly and sensually, a promise in them that he intended her to feel. He still held her hands in one of his above her head. "Okay?"

"Yeah, all green."

"Good girl."

She kept her eyes closed, which made it easier to use the element of surprise to wrap the soft silk scarf he had showed her gently around her wrists. He didn't anchor them to anything. This was going to be a lesson in self-control for both of them. He sensed her bewilderment as she tentatively moved her hands and found she could if she really wanted to.

"Oh, my love, one day I hope I'll have you spread out and tied down for me so you have to look and enjoy," he said huskily, "but today, I need to let you realize you can trust. Okay?"

She nodded.

"Vocalize, please, love."

"Eh?" Vairi sounded startled. "Oh, er, yeah, sure. It's all good."

"Thank the gods," Raig said, his words heartfelt. "For I tell you this, if those magic fingers of yours touch me again, I'll come before I start. This is experience, not touch, for you. Lie there for me, let me feast my eyes on your amazing body while you discover all those sensations running through you. Tell me *what* you feel, *how* you feel, what you like. Let me know how you would like me to touch you, let me learn all I can about you."

"Can I watch?" Her voice was thin and reedy.

"Soon," he promised as he got back on the bed, the mattress dipping as he straddled her, took one hard nipple into his mouth and sucked.

She moaned in enjoyment.

"You like that?" He treated the other nipple to the same attention as she nodded.

"It's like you're sending awareness straight to my clit," she replied frankly. "I want more. Touch and taste, Rake, let me show you how you make me feel. Fill me, so I can discover what it is like to feel you deep inside me."

Raig trailed a series of tiny kisses down her body before he blew softly on her overheated pussy.

"Sheesh, that is…" She stopped speaking as her body clenched and relaxed. "Hmm, mmm…mmmmm." Her voice trailed off into a sound like a happy puppy would make.

"Oh, I'll do more than that, my Vairi," he vowed. "Open your eyes if you want and watch."

Obviously she wanted—she opened them. He knew all the passion he felt showed in his expression and hoped she could recognize it for what it was. He moved back onto his haunches to reach her clit and suck. She arched off the bed and into him.

"I'm going to come," Vairi said in a staccato burst of words. "Got to. Now…"

He agreed. "Eventually, but not yet. Listen well. You will not come until I say so, now will you?"

"Eh? Oh shit, I—"

"Won't come until I say so." He made sure there was no room for doubt in his voice. "Understand, love." He nipped and nibbled around her belly button as he slid a finger into her. "You'll be screaming my name before long, love. Loud, very loud. I'm going to fill you over and over. Spill my seed into you, come so hard, and make you do the same. But not until I say so. Are you hot and ready for me?"

"For fuck's sake, I'm so ready I'm buzzing. Without anything electrical to sound the buzz," she said bluntly and vehemently.

Huh? Oh, he got it. "No need for a vibrator, I'll vibrate you."

"Good. Well, please do it then. I've held back as well as I can, but shit, Raig, I'm wet with wanting. Come into me and in me. Now." Her legs moved restlessly, opening wide, her body lifting to him in welcome, as if desperate to touch him and to feel his touch in return. She arched her tied hands in supplication in his direction. Only the knowledge that he needed to be deep inside her before he came and when she fell kept him at arm's length.

"Please, Raig."

"Oh, I please. Hell, do I." He quickly smoothed a condom on, then allowed the tip of his cock to nudge her clit before he edged slowly into her. "Ah, my Vairi, so warm and welcoming." He gave a sudden push and she opened to him, and welcomed his pulsing cock deep inside her.

"Jeez, Raig, that is so good." She was panting as he moved in and out, setting up a tempo that they both danced to. Raig used his fingers, to nip and tease her nipples as she writhed and moaned at the feelings he created for her. She joined him in his rhythm and helped him to move deeper, more surely into her pussy. Even though her wrists were tied together, she could still move forward, the loop of material linking her hands giving her a chance to hook it around his neck and pull him down toward her. Raig moved willingly as they danced in unison, their cadence as old as time, his movements confident and true, definite and positive as he filled her, and used his dexterous fingers to touch and caress either her nipples or her clit.

This was more than fucking, was so much more than mere sex. He hoped she realized that.

"Shit, Raig, now. Please, please, now." Vairi screamed when her climax overtook her, and Raig could only join her as they were flung into a vortex so powerful he had no idea how or where it would end. Dimly, he heard his shout echo hers as he met her in that state of satiation. His own groan of ecstasy and completion mimicked hers and he knew he had experienced what she had. Knew things would never be the same again.

Chapter Five

Gingerly, Raig levered himself upward and lifted his body from where he had collapsed on her after his climax.

"Hmmph?" Vairi mumbled and flapped one hand in the air before she dropped it back onto the mattress with a thump. "I'm dead."

"Not quite." Squashing her was not part of Raig's plans. Romancing her, loving her and becoming a couple was. Anything more than that he dared not hope for. He pressed a swift kiss on each closed eyelid, undid the silk scarf still wrapped around her wrists and got off the bed to dispose of the condom. Vairi opened one eye to look at him in query.

"Huh?"

"Bathroom. I'll not be long."

She nodded, and the eye closed again. "'Kay."

Amused, he made certain she couldn't fail to hear the laughter in his voice. "Ah, love. Have I worn you out?"

She gave a small smile without opening her eyes. "We old women, I don't know, we just don't have the endurance to keep up with you youngsters. I need sleep. Chocolate and coffee. In any order."

"Oh now then, Vairi My Queen, I'll not be agreeing with all that there. You more than kept up with me, more than. But don't worry, we can keep practicing until I get it right. I love you." Raig was heartened to hear her make fun of something he knew bothered her. "I'll find the chocolate and coffee in a sec."

Both eyes opened. "Get what right? I thought we did pretty well."

Haha. Got you. Even if you didn't mention the 'L' word this time. Raig remembered her words spoken in the heat of the moment. He hoped with all his heart she'd meant them in the way he did.

"Oh, we did. We did supremely well. Love makes all the difference, wouldn't you say?"

"Of course it does," she replied honestly. "It adds a further dimension, because of that extra depth of feeling."

"And we felt that, did we not?" He held his breath, uncaring of how he must look, condom in one hand.

"Of cour—" She stopped mid-word and sighed. "I don't know. Oh, go and dump that in the bin, and we can analyze after if you want. Sod coffee, I can't be bothered to wait for the percolator to perk. I'm going to be very British and make tea. Do you want a cup?"

He laughed. "Yes, please, but hold on a sec." He disappeared into the bathroom, where he disposed of the condom, and after washing himself, dampened another cloth before going back into the bedroom. Vairi hadn't moved, and he tenderly ran it over her still-swollen pussy, eliciting a sharp gasp—not one of pain, he hoped.

"There now." With a swift kiss, he saluted her before he pulled her up and tapped her ass. "Chocolate in the fridge."

Vairi moaned and went limp, presumably in protest of his tap. "Heartless creature. Here I am, knackered due to you, and you're hauling me up from my bed. Cruel."

"You said you were going to make tea," he pointed out. "I'm only helping you. Still, if you're not wanting any help..." He began to let her fall back toward the bed. She shrieked.

"Don't you dare, you rotten sod." Vairi chuckled so much there was nothing she could do to stop herself bouncing as he dropped her gently back onto the mattress. "Bugger."

Looking down at her as she laughed up at him, all flushed and happy, Raig knew his heart was in his eyes, showing exactly what she meant to him. He felt himself falling as she sneaked out a hand to touch his bum and set him off balance by hooking her ankle around his leg. He landed on his stomach next to her.

"Ha! Gotcha." Vairi sounded triumphant.

He grinned. "Not totally knackered then, my love?" He went to get up. A hand in the small of his back kept him firmly where he was. The mattress moved, then—sweet Lord—she moved so her soft legs brushed either side of his body and her hands gently massaged his back. His breath caught as he Vairi sat on his ass with care. She moved up and down and her pubic hair brushed him as to reach his shoulders and neck. The sensations were amazing. Her long hair swept over him and her hands alternated the pressure of the strokes on his body.

Vairi gave a sensuous sigh, as her pussy rubbed against him and elicited enticing and promising responses. Raig let himself be caught up in the maelstrom.

Totally relaxed as he was, the sharp slap to his ass caught him by surprise. *What the fuck?* Vairi had swung to one side and moved off him enough to be able to administer it.

"Tea." There was happiness in her voice, he was sure of it. "Just thought I'd make sure you weren't stiff in all the wrong places."

"Well then, you've surely succeeded, my Vairi. You can do that at any time. Are you a masseuse?" He rolled over to look at her before sitting up and taking hold of one of her hands and sliding his fingers over the palm. "Magic hands, my love. Thank you." He kissed the spot he'd touched and curled her fingers over it. "There now, to keep it safe."

"Thank you." She spoke so softly Raig had to strain to hear her. Her voice increased in volume. "Okay, now it's cup-of-tea time. And that chocolate if you've actually got any."

Moving to a tall cabinet, Raig then opened it and threw her a different dressing gown before dragging on a pair of joggers. He had to keep a hold on his sanity and that other enticing—on her—robe wouldn't have helped. "I'm sure there'll be something to keep your strength up." He watched her thread her arms into the once again overlong sleeves, turning them up several times before tying the belt tight around her waist. Although it came just below the knee on him, it was ankle-length on Vairi. He thought it was very sexy and made her look vulnerable. That was something he was fairly sure didn't apply to his Vairi. He was wise enough not to speak his thoughts out loud.

"Come on then, woman, where's that tea you keep promising me?" His eyes were bright as he took her hand and walked the few steps to the kitchen. "There's one thing about a trailer—nowhere is very far from you," he commented as he rummaged in the fridge and watched her unconsciously sensual movements as she filled the kettle and switched it on. He found what he had been looking for and held two large bars of chocolate up to show her. "Okay, plain or milk?

"You like chocolate then?" Vairi asked mildly.

"Just a bit. Do you not?"

"Oh, I do. Unfortunately, so do my hips. They grab it and drag it straight to them. Then keep it there. So it's an indulgence. One I'm going to indulge in. Milk, please. Do you have a teapot? I couldn't find one earlier."

He shook his head. "I did, but now I don't. It came to an unfortunate end a couple of days ago, and I've not got round to getting a new one." Raig could see the question as it formed and preempted it. "I was sitting outside, enjoying some sunshine, and when I got called away I forgot about it and left it on the grass. Phil trod on it. It's on my to-do list. When I get round to making one."

"Oh well, 'yucky tea bag in a cup' tea then." Vairi suited her actions to her words and within a few minutes she handed him his mug then dropped down into the seat next to him at the table.

Raig took the drink with a few words of thanks and watched as she unwrapped the foil around her chunk of chocolate, her movements economical. Her delicate hands reminded him of earlier, and he remembered she hadn't answered his question about her profession.

"So, what do you do for a living?" he asked casually as he helped himself to a thin strip of plain chocolate.

Vairi carried on eating. Finally, she looked at him. "Work. What about you?"

Ah. A non-answer. Therefore, he gave the same answer back. "Work."

"That's all right then." Vairi finished her tea, stood and took her cup to the sink. He watched her from under hooded lids as she pushed the overlong sleeves of his dressing gown up her arms again. Even though she'd rolled them several times they had still slipped down. The excess material masked her body and damn if it didn't tease all his senses. Raig's cock show interest, and he cursed. Unfortunately, he had to get some sleep. Saturdays were busy, and he needed to be awake and alert.

"Shall we be going to bed, my love, to cuddle each other to sleep?" he asked quietly. "The alarm is going to be ringing in our ears in a couple of hours, and I'll need to be at least half with it." He saw her glance down at his joggers. Loose as they were, his cock was still making its presence known.

He grinned wryly. "Yeah, the flesh is very willing, but the spirit's trying very hard to say no. We're up and running by half ten, eleven tomorrow, and there's a good three hours' work to be done before then." He stretched, bringing his muscles into play. Vairi moved close to him and put her arm around his neck before she kissed him, long and hard.

His cock hardened and pulsed. Shit. It was no good, he needed her there and then. Sod sleep, it was overrated anyway. Raig stretched his arm out to take her wrist, but Vairi pulled away and walked into the tiny bedroom.

"I call the bathroom first." Vairi disappeared through the bathroom door, and he heard the tap being turned on. It was only a few minutes before she returned. "All yours. Any preference to which side I take?" She gestured to the bed. "And where's the other tattoos then?'

"Ahaha, I'm not telling." He shook his head and made his way into the bathroom. Too late for a shower, he decided on a wash and a brush of his teeth. He took off his pants before he went back into the bedroom and discovered Vairi had decided on where to sleep. Right in the middle. Sleep being the operative word. She was out for the count. With a grin, Raig pulled back the duvet and maneuvered her over enough to spoon in behind her. She gave an incoherent mutter. He dropped a kiss on the top of her head as he settled. "Good night, my love. Love you."

He was almost sure he discerned a soft "and you" in return before he cuddled in tightly and fell asleep. Not many hours later he woke up to the raucous noise of his alarm and groaned. Three hours' sleep was nowhere near enough, but that was what he had managed. *Get up and get over it, Raig,* he told himself as he got out of bed and moved slowly into the bathroom. Vairi, he noticed, hadn't stirred. Although how anyone could sleep through the clock's racket he had no idea. He'd once been told it could be heard three trailers down.

An almost-cold shower went a long way toward waking him up. All of him, he noticed ruefully. The barely tepid water had done nothing to diminish the morning hard-on he had sported when he woken with his cock nestling between the luscious cheeks of Vairi's butt. He dressed swiftly in an old pair of jeans, with non-designer rips over the knee and thighs and a T-shirt faded by umpteen times in the washer. Those, along with a battered pair of trainers, were perfect for the grunt work needed before the fair opened for business. Raig ran his hands through his hair, decided he really needed it cut, and that a razor had to meet his chin sooner rather than later. Rough ablutions completed, he walked through the bedroom, past a still-slumbering Vairi, and into the kitchen. By the time the kettle had boiled and he had filled the cafetière, he could hear noises from the bedroom.

Raig sensed her the moment she entered the kitchen. He turned to see her, looking to his mind much too awake for someone who had only had a few hours of sleep, never mind the exercise. He indicated the coffee.

Vairi groaned. "Mmm, please. I'm sure it was the smell of coffee that woke me up. Or perhaps it was the fact that I wasn't being pushed out of bed." Her eyes twinkled.

"Not out of bed, love, never. Maybe I was just cuddling."

"Could be." She moved into him for a kiss. "Well, good morning. What have you to do today?"

Briefly he outlined his day's work—long, hard and physical. "And as I've a feeling I'll have to kick Jonny's butt to keep him away from the carousel, I'll need to be watching him as well. So, my Vairi, what will you be doing? I can take you home now or arrange a taxi for later. Or you can stay and look around. Tonight, you could be my partner at the fair. No rides, well, not the mechanical sort anyway."

"Er, well, um, I'd better get home at some point, although I'd like a look around when it's open. But tonight? I'm sorry, Raig, I can't come to the fair. I'm busy."

He waited. She didn't elaborate, and he was damned if he was going to ask what with. Instead he nodded, took a mouthful of coffee and almost scalded himself. Raig set his cup down carefully, even though he wanted to shout and moan, throw it at the wall and drum his heels. *Like a two-year-old*, he thought, disgusted. He spoke as evenly as he could. "So, is this the big heave-ho? Wham, bam and thank you?"

She looked horrified. "No! Oh, Raig, no, it's not that. I've got a prior commitment. If you want to come for breakfast tomorrow, I'll cook you my Sunday Special." She still didn't elaborate.

He got the idea that he could wait until Sunday, and she still wouldn't tell him any more. He couldn't call her for keeping secrets because he hadn't exactly been as open as he could. *Build a bridge and get over it.*

"Deal. What is the 'Sunday Special'? Do you cook it naked?" He made his voice hopeful.

She laughed. "In your dreams, Rake O'Shea. I don't want hot splatters on my anything. Although maybe a frilly apron could be accommodated, as long as you do the same for me sometime. With a tea towel maybe?"

Now that conjured up interesting ideas. As well as an interested cock. "I'm thinking that idea has possibilities now," he said, his brogue strong. "So I'll be looking forward to our creativity. What time will you be wanting me to come?" At her quizzical look, he added, "For breakfast."

She smiled and laughed. "I'll be happy to oblige, anytime."

"I'll remember that."

Vairi drank her coffee as she looked at him over the top of her mug.

Speculating.

Now what? This woman, this amazing, intriguing, gorgeous woman was going to have to accept sooner rather than later just what she meant to him. And understand what he meant to her.

"Why are you looking at me as if I've grown horns?" he asked with interest.

Her eyes drifted down to his crotch and back up again. "Ah, is that what it is?"

"Tease."

She nodded. "Yup. So do I get a guided tour? I need to be away by midafternoon, but I'll wander into town for an hour if you can spare time for me later on this morning."

"For you? I'll make time." He put his mug into the sink and slopped water over it before he left it on the drainer. Even that was more than he usually managed on a Saturday morning. "Everything should be running before eleven, so if I come back for you then?" He dried his hands on a scrap of towel.

Vairi nodded.

"Help yourself to anything you want, although I think my boxers might be a bit large." Raig winked. "Mind you it'll put some very interesting scenarios in my mind and help me get through the next few hours."

"Oh, bragging, are we? I have nice, clean" — she bent forward and lowered her voice — "sexy undies. I'm not saying I'll be wearing them, but I've definitely got them." She paused and leaned away. "If I go out, will I be able to get back in?"

In answer he opened a cupboard above his head and took out a small pouch. "Trailer keys. Right, I'd best be off before I'm accused of slacking. I'll meet you here as near to eleven as I can make it." He kissed her long and lingering and, as ever, had the body-clenching reaction of his nipples turning as hard as iron and his cock rock-solid and fighting his jeans to be contained. *Hell, Raig, go before you come. And don't say that out loud, for the Lord's sake.*

"Later, love." He whistled cheerfully as he swung out of the door and walked briskly across the dew-dampened grass to the Ready Room. Phil had beaten him to it.

"Well," his manager observed. "You looked fucked. Well and truly. Not get much sleep?" He was amused and it showed.

"Yes, yes and no." Raig looked him in the eyes and covered his mouth as he yawned. "There will be no comments. No jokes, no fooling. She is important. I never believed Da about how he felt when he met Ma, and now I do. I just need to make Vairi understand she does as well."

"Good luck." Phil's tone was sympathetic.

Raig nodded. "I'll be thanking you because I've a feeling it'll be needed. Now what's to be done?" He tried to put Vairi out of his mind and concentrate on work. He was partially successful. The curve of a globe on the side of a stall reminded him of the curve of her breast as she lay on her side, the color of a backcloth the shade of her eyes. A laugh by one of the stallholders reminded him of her laughing down at him as he rose above her. *Raig, my lad, you've got it bad.* Every bloody thing reminded him of her.

It was just after eleven when he returned to his trailer. Vairi was sitting on the steps, chatting to Jonny. Raig almost stopped in his tracks. The surge of jealousy he felt when he saw them laughing together rocked him. Then she looked at him and smiled, and the green-eyed monster in him dissipated. Whether she knew it or not, that look spoke of love and togetherness.

"Jonny's been keeping me company." Vairi stood and brushed her hands down her jeans as she did so. Jonny grinned. "Telling me all your secrets..."

Raig's heart missed a beat.

Jonny doesn't know. No one except his close-knit TV team did.

"More like she's been stopping me from trying to work like you wanted. She's a clever one, your woman, Raig. Even wanted to know where your tattoos were."

Raig saw her eyes flash and stepped in before Jonny found out what it was like to be on the receiving end of her clever tongue and be scarred for life. "Then I'll be thanking her, Jonny, for you'll not be going anywhere near the rides or the stalls today, or it'll be me you answer to. Understand? And I'll be lookin' forward to my Vairi finding the tattoos herself." There was enough of a hard tone in his voice for Jonny to register the intent and know he was serious about all he said.

Jonny sighed and Raig relented slightly.

"You can go to the Ready Room this evening if you really want to, but until then you stay in or around the trailers. Okay?" He looked steadily at Jonny until he nodded.

"Good. Right, I'm off to show Vairi around. I'll catch you later." He swung Vairi up off the step and gave her a deep kiss. As ever, his cock showed immediate interest and reluctantly moved her away from him. "Let's go." He encouraged her across the grass to where the fair was waking up.

Two hours later, he was disgruntled and didn't really know why. Unless it had something to do with a massive, rock-hard erection and an incipient need to screw his lady senseless. Vairi had charmed everyone he had introduced her to, looked deliberately vague at the innuendo and sharp cracks bandied around, then with a hug and a kiss left him with the comment, "Breakfast any time after nine."

He watched as she got into the taxi and was driven away. Something bugged him, but he was damned if he knew what it was. Meanwhile he had work to do.

Half an hour or so later his phone vibrated. *Is it Vairi? Has she changed her mind about the evening?* Eagerly he fished it out. Groaned when he saw Denny's name flash up. *Time to face the music.*

"Hi, Denny, how's it going?" There was an indignant squawk on the other end of the line. *Shit, fuck and all other epithets, it isn't Denny, but Lorna.* "No, no, I don't know. Lorna, for fuck's sake, ask her."

"I did." The voice sounded well pissed off.

Shit, he didn't need the phone to catch what she said, she was yelling loud enough for the whole site to hear. He checked he wasn't on loud speaker. He wasn't.

"She said you spent all night having red-hot sex, the best she's ever had. Told me she was now a fully paid-up cougar. You bastard, how could you do that to my mum? Red-hot sex."

"Well, if you don't know how red-hot sex works, Denny is not the man I thought he was." Raig was exasperated and let it show. "Hello, Lorna. Your mum is a big girl now. If she says that's what we did all night, that is what we did."

"But she's my mum," Lorna wailed. "I can't get the picture out of my mind that my mum…you…stuff."

He laughed. "Double standards or what, Lorna? Seriously, she's well able to stand up for herself. You asked me to show her a good time. I'm thinking I did that. Right enough of this. I've got to go." He cut the call. *Red-hot sex, eh? Nice one.* Raig remembered Lorna's indignation and smirked. *None of your business*, he thought as he continued his inspection of the site. *Tough if your idea had reared up and bitten you on the bum. Maybe she would think twice about interfering with other people's lives in the future.*

Maybe. Ten minutes later, his pocket was vibrating again just as he was finishing his conversation with the stallholder of hook-a-duck. He had smiled as he approached, remembering Vairi's comments. He took out his phone. As he had supposed, it was Vairi. Had she had the indignant phone call? It seemed she had.

"Honestly, Rake. How old do they think I am?" she asked in exasperation, even though humor colored her voice. "I got hell because I'd not rung her. Why I needed to ring her, I haven't got a clue. Hell again, because I pointed out they set us up. Then I evidently added insult to injury, because when she asked me what we'd been up to I said 'red-hot sex'. And I'm running late, but I just wanted to warn you, you'll more than likely get a phone call. Tell her to mind her own business. Now gotta fly, see you in the morning." The line went dead before he had a chance to ask "fly where, and why".

Raig shook his head, amused at how one night had fired up so many peoples' emotions. So where was the call from Denny then? It didn't materialize. Just a text, with 'Oh ho, I'm in shit. Keep your head down'. He was too busy to do anything else. Dog-tired and irritable. It had been one of those days. The dodgems' generator failed, and some arsehole had smashed over a dozen lights around the coconut shy with several badly aimed balls. A lost child was eventually found under a tarpaulin, although not before the police had been alerted, and someone had tried to take the cash from the candy floss stall, only to be head butted by the five-foot-nothing octogenarian called Wendy who ran it. The wannabe thief was persuaded not to press charges for Wendy's so-called assault, because, as he was told between hoots of laughter, no one would believe him.

Eventually he sat in the Ready Room with Phil and waited as Jonny got them all a beer from the fridge in the tiny attached kitchen. He heard an exclamation, a burst of noise and a "yee-ha". He raised an eyebrow to Phil, who shrugged. "Jonny listening to the radio."

The noise got louder. Jonny pushed open the door, three bottles in one hand and a radio in the other.

"Needed." Raig drank deeply. "What a day."

"Don't you mean what a last night?" Jonny inquired slyly, and Phil laughed as Raig held his bottle in the air as a toast.

"And that as well, though in very different ways. I am knackered. In every which way."

"Stop bragging." Jonny switched the radio louder before sitting in a chair and crossing his booted feet. "We need to listen to this program. Eddy Nelson, the lorry driver, told me about it. Says it's funny, sexy and damn good. I got the last half hour last week. It was all about eunuchs. And apricots, though not together."

"Thank God, you had me worried." Phil held up his bottle in a salute. "Fine then, let's listen. Okay with you, Raig?"

He nodded. "If I fall asleep, it's not because I don't think the company is scintillating, I just can't stay awake. Who's the host?" He wasn't really interested, asking more for the sake of staying in the conversation.

The radio told him before anyone else.

"Hello. Midnight already, and it's me again, Cracking Carry C with Saturday Night Sounds, for all you people of the night. Before I get going, did any of you watch the TV program about the exposes of those sex traders? Really informative. I hope they don't do what they threatened to the intrepid reporter. We need more like him. It's no wonder we only know him as the Irishman eh? Bet he's really a cockney. Anyway, I just want to dedicate this first song to him, because, as he said, that's how he first got a hint of what was going on. So, to the Irishman, workers, insomniacs and lovers of good music and chat—boy, do I have all that and more tonight—let's start off with Marvin Gaye and *I Heard it Through the Grapevine*. Because tonight, our grapevine is full of fruit." The instantly recognizable notes filled the room.

Witty, Raig thought, as he tried to conjure up an image of the seductive-sounding Carry C. However, all he could see was an image of Vairi, her voice talking to him. And she'd seen his programs in the past? That was interesting. Pity he couldn't ask her more about how she felt. But then he knew more than anyone that he had to keep a low — as in invisible — profile. The people he exposed wouldn't think twice about putting him in the foundations of a motorway bridge. *Man, you've got it bad*, he told himself. The music died away and he had to force himself to sit back and relax instead of straining forward as if the radio could give up her secrets. He saw Phil looking at him with a smile, Jonny openly laughing.

"Sexy voice, eh?"

He nodded, took another mouthful of beer and a handful of crisps from the bowl on the table. Anything to stop him opening his mouth and putting his feet in it with banal comments. He listened as she began speaking again. She did sound like Vairi, just after she came. Interesting.

"Well, people, Stevie has just saved the evening with a chocolate croissant and a large, extra-shot cappuccino. I've been a wee bitty busy today, and I need my caffeine. I told him if his wife ever gets fed up of him leaving wet towels on the bed and boots him out, he can become my official coffee maker any time." She chuckled throatily and Jonny moaned.

"Man, what that does to me."

"Down, boy," Phil said and Raig groaned humorously. He felt the same way. Was he getting the hots for an unseen, unknown woman, just because she sounded like Vairi? *Sick, Raig, sick.*

"Er, maybe I'd better explain, to any of my new listeners, his wife is my best friend, and we've been friends since primary school. Him and wet towels are her bugbear." Carry C laughed, deeply and soulfully. "Ah, bless, he's gutted I only want him for his coffee-making skills. Evidently he makes a mean bacon sarnie as well. Never experienced that. Now, enough of Stevie and on to my week." There was a violin playing softly in the background. Raig was half sure he had heard the music recently. Whatever. He was reacting to it. Not the best thing with his two friends in the room and ready to comment.

"So," she spoke as the violins faded. "What a week it's been. Super injunctions being bypassed. Harry Seville marrying for the fifth time, my producer swearing off pot noodles — again. And the fair in town. Guaranteed to give you the ride of your life. Any comments on any of this week's news, just email them to us. Although talking of *rides*…" She paused, and Raig cracked up. Talk about innuendo. He couldn't understand how Jonny and Phil didn't know exactly what she was talking about, but by their expressions of interest but not enlightenment he guessed they didn't.

"Anyway," she continued. "I have a dilemma to put to you. Is it perfectly acceptable for an older woman to go out with a younger man? Like lots of years? More than ten. I have a friend who wants to know. So, listeners, Friends of the Night, what do you think? You have the email address, let's try to help her. Whilst we're doing that, here's Fairground Attraction and *Perfect*." The music increased and her voice faded.

"We're on the radio." Phil chuckled after the first few bars sounded loud in the room. "We should play this more often over the rides, it's a good one. I wonder who wants to know all about an older woman and a younger man, eh?" He looked meaningfully at Raig, who ignored him, his suspicions of Cracking Carry C increasing every minute.

Jonny snorted. "I seem to know someone who sort of might have some answers there, eh, Raig?'

Raig shrugged. "Bad grammar, Joh, very bad. Your ma would ask where all that education went." He laughed and ducked Jonny's swat in his direction. "I've no idea, but it'll be interesting to hear the replies, eh? Anyone want a refill?" Anything to get a few seconds alone so he could adjust his boner and regulate his breathing.

As he stood, the voice on the radio intruded. "Well, now lots of emails coming in. First, we'll have this request, then we'll have a chat." The voice dropped slightly, becoming full of intrigue and desire. "So, this is for a rake — *Takin' Care of Business*."

Chapter Six

"Oh, Raig, was she saying that for you?" Jonny teased. "I wonder what business is being taken care of."

Raig shook his head in amusement. "Who'd want to play a request for me? Though with a voice like that, I hope it's her." *And I hope she's who I think she is.*

"Probably looks nothing like her voice suggests," Phil offered. "Ninety, saggy boobs and a cat called Maude. Smells of mothballs and mint imperials."

Raig took the lifeline. "More than likely." He finished his beer in one mouthful. "Right, I'm off. Enjoy the rest of your beer. Late start tomorrow. I'll see you around four, Phil. Ring if you need me. Jonny, before you ask, yes, you can work tomorrow if you feel up to it." With a brief good night, he left the other two. Even before the trailer door had swung shut behind him, he had his phone out of his pocket and the radio app switched on. He headed across the fairground, nodding to the ever-present security staff he passed. Out here the voice was less clear and more distorted, but even so, he would bet his last thousand he had heard it not twenty-four hours earlier. Those same husky tones drugged with passion and shouting his name, screaming in ecstasy as excitement and sexual satiation overwhelmed its owner.

"So, keep those emails coming in," the tinny voice said throatily. "Lots of you have enjoyed the fair. Kelly says it brings out the child in all of us. Although she's no longer sick through eating too much candy floss and doughnuts. Morag says she and her boyfriend enjoyed the rides. I must say I really enjoyed the ride I had."

Raig sputtered. Surely others must pick up on the innuendo. It had to be Vairi. As soon as he reached his trailer, he turned on his digital radio and headed for his laptop. Carry C was due another email. He was sure this one would not be read out. Raig would have loved to have been a fly on the wall when she'd read it. Brief and succinct—

You can ride me anytime. Older women — well, one older woman — rules. Remember, you are only as old as (what/who) you feel.

He poured himself a dram of the fine single malt he treated himself to every time he headed north of the border and added the correct amount of water while he waited to discover what would happen next. It wasn't long before he found out.

"Well, peeps, here's some very interesting comments. A lot of emails tonight, and some requests. Some possible, alas, some not. One particularly was very helpful for my friend. Raig, thank you for your advice, I'll be sure to make sure she listens to it. Raig says older women rule, and we are only as old as we feel. That's very reassuring. And he's offered to take me for a ride. That's nice." Her voice was deliberately bland. "So is this next track. It's *Human* by The Killers. All the oldies tonight, as I'm in a mellow mood. It's dance around the radio time."

Raig spluttered whisky as he laughed out loud. How wrong could a bloke be? Damn if he wasn't enjoying this. He wondered if the emails were making her blush, or hot and bothered. He planned for it to be the latter. This email was short and to the point—

I'd rather feel you.

It was followed seconds later by another.

On another note, do you like pancakes?

He wandered around the trailer, unable to settle. Whether Carry C — Vairi — was hot and bothered or not, he was.

"Oh, now I so love that track. Great for exercising to."

Oh shit. Now all he could think about was Vairi's gorgeous breasts jiggling about as she bounced to that song.

"So," the honey-toned voice continued. "Let's read some more of these emails. Stevie, my producer, was just saying what a lot of interest my older woman query has generated. He and Andie are reading them as fast as they can, but I doubt we'll get through them all. However, Darren says his wife is eleven years older than him, and he loves her more each day. Way to go, Darren. Jenny and Clive say as long as its legal, it's fine. Oh ho, Mary says no older woman wants to be bothered with a younger bloke. Well, all I can say there, Mary, is sorry, but it looks like you're wrong, judging by the bulk of the emails." She laughed and that throaty sound went straight to Raig's cock and into his balls. 'All wound up and raring to go' was an understatement.

"Now, on the subject of super injunctions, Alex emailed to say 'why should you be allowed to be naughty and not get talked about just because you are rich? Don't we live in a democracy, freedom of speech and all that? If I cheated and got found out, all my friends, neighbors, and colleagues would know'," Carry C said. "Well, he's got a point there. One that a lot of you agree with. So we should be thanking The Irishman and his investigating, eh? I think we could keep tonight's subjects rolling for longer than we've got. However, it's time for some more music."

Ah, he hadn't thought about others reading the messages. With an inward smirk, he composed his next one. To her producer.

Hope you are enjoying these as much as we are. Please remind Vairi not to forget the maple syrup.

There, that should give this Stevie guy something to talk about. And it seemed her. *Way to go, Vairi*, he thought as he listened to her reply.

"Ah, I've just been reminded I'm making pancakes tomorrow." He could hear amusement in her voice. "I've got to remember the maple syrup. Now I ask you, who wouldn't already have a jar in the pantry? Well, unless you're a sugar and lemon or chocolate spread person. Me? I just love chocolate spread all over." The voice dripped with suggestion. "So, toppings. What's your favorite? Drop us an email and let us know. Stevie likes coffee over anything. He must do, he's just choked and sprayed it everywhere. Andie says chocolate every time. Preferably chocolate orange. Mmm, now there's a thought. Let's hear from you. Favorite toppings and older — or younger — men. Not necessarily together. Let's have your views. Now here's Shaz Doley, a lovely local girl, who I predict will be big with *Mind Over Matter*."

Her innuendos brought tears to his eyes. Never before had he sat by himself and laughed until he cried and his ribs hurt. Time for a few 'her eyes only' messages. He hoped she would appreciate them. Thank god they'd exchanged phone numbers.

Never thought I could get off on a voice, but…

He didn't sign it until the next text. Then only with a simple,

R xxx.

Before following it with,

I could do if…

He had to curb his impatience between texts to give her a chance to read them in order —

You were here in person, guiding me. As it is…
I'll wait until that happens. But…

A little helping hand will have to keep me going, although…

Only if I know you'll help yourself when you read this… therefore…

Do we have a deal? Is your hand straying?

I'm thinking of you, so is my cock.

It's saying my hand is a poor substitute, but…

Let me imagine you're helping yourself to stay wet.

Put those magic fingers inside you…

And on your clit…

Ah, Vairi My Queen, what I wouldn't do to see you make yourself come.

Maybe one day?

Oh, my love, I'm so hard, horny and fucking frustrated. So ready for you.

I've stopped.

I'm not coming until I'm hard and tight inside you.

Fuck, I ache.

Still, only a few hours to go.

I'll bring the maple syrup in case you're out…

Or is it chocolate sauce?

Night, my love. Sleep tight.

"Okay, Vairi. Let's see what you make of that." Now all he had to do was try to sleep before he saw her again. He didn't have a lot of success.

* * * *

Raig was awake and up at silly o'clock. He'd slept so little, and when he had it had been so fragmented, that it made no sense to stay in bed and twist and turn. Therefore, it was barely nine when he knocked on Vairi's door. Much too early. Although, had they set a time? He hadn't been able to remember, but after he'd spent a good hour wandering around aimlessly he'd decided he wasn't prepared to wait any longer. If she wasn't up, he'd camp on her doorstep until she was.

"It's open," she yelled. "Come on in."

What? What planet is she on, leaving the door unlocked? Had she even locked it earlier? Didn't we have a conversation about this before? Surely she knows there are weirdoes about everywhere these days?

He frowned as he entered the kitchen. Even the sight of her, dressed in another floaty outfit with delicate silk ties all the way down the front that invited him to pull each one open and discover what was underneath, didn't distract him from his annoyance for long.

"Hi, you. What's up?"

Her gaze drifted downward, and even though he was grouchy, his cock responded predictably and perked up. Her next words annoyed him.

"Lost a tenner and found a quid?"

"Why on earth is the door unlocked?" he asked irritably and ignored her humorous question. "Shouting for me to come in. Honestly, woman, I can't believe you're so stupid. For goodness' sake, I could have been anyone."

Oh ho, stupid yourself, Raig. Her eyes, which a few seconds before had been lingering on his crotch, helping his cock to be 'up', were now flashing fire.

"Well, my bad luck it was you then." She went back to cracking eggs into a bowl and ignored him. Raig slammed the door behind him and glared at her.

"Sorry."

"Say it as if you mean it or don't say it at all." Vairi stared at him for a long moment, shrugged and obviously decided not to comment further. Instead she ignored his obvious temper and just carried on cooking. Was checking the bacon hadn't burned and the herbed tomatoes were grilling to perfection more important than responding?

"However, it's accepted. Scrambled okay?" she asked pleasantly. "It should be, as it will mimic your brain."

You what? Raig was stunned into silence. Then he laughed. A big, full-bodied belly laugh. "Ouch. Was I being a bit of a Neanderthal then, my Vairi?"

"Mmm," she said drily. "You could say that. Stomped in,

no 'good morning, hi, how are you', just moaning. Lovely way to start the day, I don't think. Here." She thrust a handful of silverware and the condiment set at him. "Set the table, lose the frown, find a smile and come back and start again."

"Yes, ma'am." He patted her butt as he walked past and put the crockery in a heap on the table.

Vairi shook her head. "Men."

He marched determinedly toward her. Took the whisk from her and cradled her face in his hands. He used his tongue to trace her lips before teasing them apart and drawing her into a long, lingering sensual kiss.

"I...am...so...sorry." He punctuated each word with a deep, drugging kiss. "I love you, my Vairi, and went cold when you shouted 'come in' like that. I hadn't announced myself. I could have been an ax murderer or a stalker or something."

She returned each kiss with enthusiasm. "We're a bit short on ax murderers and stalkers around here. I need to scramble the eggs, or the bacon will be eggless."

"Mmm, never mind." He nuzzled her neck. "No eggs, no bacon, no matter. No kisses does matter."

Laughing, she moved his hands and turned to the cooker. "I bet you won't say that if I tell you it's toast, toast, or, er, toast for breakfast. Now give me five minutes and we can eat."

"Five, three, whatever. Although I do have a question. What happened to pancakes? No syrup?"

She turned toward him, a spatula in her hands, and made threatening gestures with it. "All things come to those who wait, including pancakes. They're for later. I needed a fry-up. Now let me concentrate. Do *not* talk about pancakes and syrup."

"Yes, ma'am. Not yet anyway. Just one more kiss to keep me going." He was as good as his word. "Now, anything else I can do?"

"Yes, set the table. And don't throw me that 'what on

earth do you mean' face. You know exactly what I mean. A guddle of knives and forks on the table does not mean it is set."

He watched her try to stop her lips from twitching, as he heaved a very over-the-top sigh and muttered something about loving a masterful woman.

"Oh," she raised her voice, "and tell me now, before I get distracted again and forget to ask you, how you knew Carry C was me."

"Your hot as hell, sexy 'come to bed and fuck me' voice. Well that's how I hear it anyway. Hopefully no one else does."

She chuckled. "Nope. I mainly get asked if I have a sore throat."

"Thank god." He swiftly set the table. "There we go."

"Spot on." Vairi nodded and grinned. "Now you've got it. So if you are very good, maybe I'll show you just how masterful I can be."

"Oh, I'll be good. Very, very, good. I'm holding you to that." He looked down at his jeans. "All of me is looking forward to holding you. What are you going on about under your breath? It's the height of bad manners to talk to yourself and not let me hear." His smiled to show he wasn't serious.

She looked flustered. "Oh, nothing, as you said, just muttering to myself."

Raig smirked as she finished cooking and plated their meals.

"Coffee in percolator, milk in insulated jug. Mugs in that cupboard." She pointed then put the plates on the table before adding the percolator and milk. Raig collected the mugs and moved across to her.

"That's yours," Vairi said and indicated the plate with the most food on it. "Tuck in."

He nodded his thanks and took the seat opposite her. "I hope you'll be rubbing your feet up my legs while we eat, Vairi My Queen."

"Nope. Eat your breakfast before it gets cold. Then maybe I'll rub my feet up your legs. Maybe."

"Woman, you're cruel. First of all, I had no Vairi in my bed last night. Then she chatted about us on the air. After that, talking to herself and excluding me from the conversation. Now she won't even rub her feet up my legs. Cruel."

"Yup." Vairi rolled her eyes, crossed them and giggled. "Cruel and heartless, that's what Lorna used to say when she didn't get her own way as well. Still does for all I know. And, in my defense, I didn't chat about us per se. I chatted in general. That's what I do. If you can't hack it, then, well, tough I guess." She poured two mugs of coffee before she picked up her cutlery and began to eat. He noted that there was a tension about her that made him conscious of how much hinged on his answer. It seemed she was more interested than she had admitted. He ate some food before putting down his knife and fork.

"Okay, let's get the elephant in the room out and on its way. I *can* hack it. As long as you can hack mine." Although he spoke quietly and with sincerity, he didn't elaborate. "I was gobsmacked last night when I realized it was you. Oh-so-fucking proud. My Vairi, you were awesome. You are awesome. Sorry I was such an ass earlier. It's hard for me not to be. I love you, and want to know you're safe." He watched and waited for her to respond. "No comment?"

Vairi poured more coffee before answering him. What she said threw him off center enough not to work out until much later that she'd chosen not to address the 'love' part of his statement. He'd been as open as he could. Would she respond in kind?

"I'd only just unlocked it. I am safety conscious, honestly. I even bought more condoms yesterday."

He stared at her before the allusion sank in. Humor flooded his face. "Flavored?" he asked wickedly.

"No, damn it." Vairi was laughing now. "You're lucky I remember what the box even looks like. Apart from that box of condoms I brought to you, which I was amazed were in date, it's been a long time since I've needed to ask for something for the weekend!"

It was Raig's turn to laugh. "I've not heard that expression for a while. I'll get flavored ones next time then, shall I?"

Vairi looked at him in bewilderment. "Is there any point? I might take you into my mouth and enjoy it, but I'm not taking a condom into my mouth, flavored or not. It's still flavored rubber. Ugh, no thanks. Don't bother to offer me colored ones either. No point when once they're on and in, you don't see them. If you do check 'em out once they are on it could scar a woman for life. A purple-spotted penis or a cherry-red cock. Doesn't bear thinking about." She shuddered in a theatrical manner. "Thin 'flesh-colored, let the sensation flow through', as the advert says. They'll do."

"Indeed they will." Raig stood and gathered their cutlery and crockery before taking it to the sink. "Drink your coffee, love, and I'll wash up. After all, if we want to try your purchases..." He winked. "We need to, what is it they say, let our food digest?"

"How many of them do you intend to try, for goodness' sake?"

He schooled his expression to one of innocence. "All of them."

She did a Stevie and sprayed coffee everywhere. Raig moved swiftly toward her and patted her on the back as she coughed and spluttered.

"There I was thinking it was your producer who you said likes coffee everywhere, not you."

In answer, she flicked some of rapidly cooling coffee at him. "I'll tell him you like the idea. About time I wound him up. He had a great session last night with your emails, was full of it when he cottoned on you knew who I was. I nearly died when he asked me oh-so-innocently if you realized he was reading them and hoped you didn't because he might get some juicy gossip to relay to Lizzie." She was chuckling as she spoke. "They've been telling me to get my libido working again for ages. That's the worst of still being friends with someone who knows all about your misspent youth. I say I'm steady and reliable. They say stuffy and reliable, and I've left my sexual awareness in the washing machine with the washing. Stevie told me last night I've obviously got the washing up to date."

He grinned before giving her a smoldering glance that had a blush suffusing her face. At least he hoped that was the reason. "Nice to know you're so prepared, Girl Guide. I'll think of some, er, interesting emails for your next program, which is when?"

"Wednesday."

"Loads of time then."

She looked at him in bewilderment. "What for?"

He moved and put her over his shoulder in a fireman's lift. "This."

Chapter Seven

"You idiot," Vairi said, though there was no heat in her words.

Her hair brushed his back and her arms dangled against his legs as he swung her from side to side.

"Raig, put me down."

He lowered her feet back on the floor. "Your wish. Well, partly." Before she had a chance to say or do anything else, he kissed her thoroughly. An unnerving suspicion had been growing steadily ever since he'd met Vairi. There was a lot he needed to tell her. Some of it she might not like and some he really shouldn't share. Nevertheless, he reasoned, as she meant so much to him—if as he planned he began to mean more to her—she had to know the problems that could arise.

Such as a bullet between my shoulders?

Unusually for him, he was procrastinating. In his life, he met everything head-on, open and clear. Because he wasn't sure how Vairi would react to his confessions, he was delaying them. For the first time ever, he was afraid the price he might have to pay was going to be too high.

Sod it, he'd worry about opening up later. He wanted *her* opened up, he thought crudely. Anywhere. "Vairi, I'm wanting to taste you. Here or wherever, your choice. But please be bloody quick in choosing. I'm telling you that kitchen table is calling to me."

She raised an eyebrow. "You might want to lock the door and close the curtains then. Just in case Lorna and Denny take it into their minds to visit. Especially after I told her she'd set me up, so she could have no complaints about what happens. It wouldn't surprise me if she doesn't turn up at some point and demand to know what's going on."

Raig remembered his phone call from Lorna. Best not to mention *that* to Vairi. He heard a car door slam somewhere nearby. Vairi groaned.

"Told you so."

"Too late?" he asked wryly.

She agreed. "Much too late. We haven't even got time to run and hide in the understairs cupboard. No windows," she added as he looked at her blankly. "Right, Mr. Showman, it's show time." Footsteps rounded the house. "In the kitchen, love," she spoke louder than before. "Come right on in. I'll make more coffee." He saw her eyes roam over him, as she caressed his erection through his jeans and one bare foot swept over his feet. "And well, let's give her food for thought, eh? She'll think you were here all night."

"If I'd been here all night, we would still be in bed," he replied frankly. "Then she would have been in for a shock."

"She'll be in for one now." Vairi smiled wickedly as she moved closer to him, her breast brushing his chest and her mouth next to his. Raig got the message, toed off his shoes and shoved them out of view under the table so he was standing barefoot before capturing her mouth with his. He hadn't meant to take hold of and caress her breast, but his hand moved of its own volition. She reached around him to cup and fondle his butt. Ahh, now that felt so good. He forgot they were about to have an audience, forgot everything except the sensations she was arousing.

"You reach my soul," he murmured into her mouth. "Every last iota, open and —"

"Well. Excuse us for butting in." The voice was light and sarcastic. "You did say come in. Shall we go out and knock?"

Without undue haste he felt Vairi move her lips. Not, he noticed, her hands, which were still gently roaming over the taut planes of his butt.

"No need," he heard her say huskily, the sensual tones

raising his heat level up several notches he could do without. "You're in now. Going out and knocking won't make any difference. Morning, you two. Coffee? I was just going to make another pot."

Her smile was so devilish he couldn't help but copy it. Talk about wicked, evil grin.

Lorna took a sharp breath and Denny stifled a laugh.

"Another one? How many have you had, for goodness' sake?"

"Just the one. We've only just finished breakfast. You're early today, Lorna. I thought Sunday was a day of rest and all that?" Vairi's tone was mild, but even Raig could hear the warning in it. *Butt out or else!* Slowly her hands 'butted' off his bum and he moved backward from her, not caring if his friends noticed his very obvious arousal. It would be hard to miss it if their eyes strayed below his waist. It should have felt strange, being found with the mother of a friend in a compromising position. It didn't. It felt right.

"I'll make it," he said easily. "Coffee for everyone?" He winked briefly at Vairi and gave her arm a quick squeeze. If Lorna was going to complain, they may as well make sure she had something big to complain about. He leaned in for another kiss. "Any idea where I left my shoes?"

Vairi kissed him back. With what he experienced was genuine enthusiasm and not put on for their audience.

"Nope." She sighed theatrically. "I guess they'll be somewhere around."

"In the bedroom?" Lorna asked acerbically.

He regarded her steadily. "Could be, although it's not your business, is it?" It was a statement, not a question.

She had the grace to look ashamed at her interjection. "Well, it is my mum you're…um…"

"Screwing? Fucking? Making love to?" Vairi spoke quietly, but with authority. "Like Raig said, Lorna, not your business."

"I don't want you to be hurt, Mum." Her tone was defensive. "After all, you're a lot older than Raig. Different generations and all that. Nothing could come of it."

Raig went to speak, but a signal from Vairi stopped him. If she agreed with Lorna, then he would not be responsible for his actions, and he would more than likely lose his best friend's friendship. As well as his lover.

"Could it not? Aren't all my bits in working order then? Have they atrophied due to lack of use? You hypocrite, Lorna." She poked her daughter in the chest, hard enough for Lorna to wince. "Happy to ask Raig to entertain me for the evening, not happy how he did it. It takes two to tango, you know, two to argue and make up, and two to make love. If we aren't bothered about the age difference, why should you be? Scared you'll get a stepfather your own age?"

Raig boggled at that but daren't hope she meant it. She hadn't finished with her daughter, however. Lorna was pale and swallowed heavily several times. "Er, Mum…"

Vairi cut her off with a sweep of her hand. "Oh no, I forgot Denny is five years older than you, and Raig a couple of years older than that. So okay. I might be a cougar, but that makes Denny almost a puma. Or is it a one-way street? Okay for him, but not for me?"

She leaned back into Raig. He had the impression that if he hadn't held her up, she'd have fallen down.

Vairi took a deep breath and exhaled noisily. "Oh, either sit down, drink your coffee and give over, or go away. I can't be bothered with all this angst." Vairi looked at her daughter steadily. Raig noticed Denny, who had still yet to speak, touch his wife's arm. Lorna stared at her mother for a few moments more, then shuddered.

"Yeah, I'm sorry. Overreaction, I guess. You know it's hard to accept your mum does 'it'." She mimed quote marks in the air. "A bit like I know now you must've felt about me doing 'it'." Again the quote marks. She looked at her mother's face. Raig decided she couldn't have been overly happy with what she saw, because she apologized again. "Mum, Raig, I am sorry. I did overreact. Denny tried to calm me down, but all I could think was it was all my fault. Even though I didn't know what this 'it' was. I was listening to your show."

"I know," Vairi said drily. "We got the email. Stevie was very amused. He decided it was perfect gossip for Lizzie."

Unexpectedly, Raig went to Lorna's rescue. "She got some from me as well, Lorna. Now she knows at least two people were listening."

Vairi punched him lightly on the arm. "Three, Lizzie always listens. I think if it hadn't been for her nagging me, I never would had said yes when Stevie put the idea of middle-aged me having a chat show and talking about all things slightly risqué, but only if you took them to be. Which reminds me, he still owes me a bottle of champagne. He dared me to talk about the time I danced on a table in a gay strip club. With his brother, I may add. Before he came out. Malcolm, I mean, not Stevie obviously."

"I never heard that. Uncle Malcolm and you in a gay strip club?" Lorna's tone showed she was unsure whether to be interested or aghast. Denny and Raig had no such inhibitions — they guffawed.

Vairi laughed with them, a sound that went straight to Raig's gut and opened up all sorts of sensations.

"That," she said with glee, "is because he forgot to add 'on air' to the dare. I told him when the show had finished. Please, don't think my life was all high living and shenanigans though. Mostly I was a happy stay-at-home mum for Lorna."

"So why were you there?" Raig was intrigued. "At the strip club. Apart from to dance on a table." He leaned forward and spoke only for her to hear. "Will you dance on a table for me sometime? Naked?"

She shook her head at him, ignored his last question and addressed his first.

"I was there as camouflage for Malcolm, because he hadn't come out. It was a, ahem, fact-finding mission for him in his role as an M.P. What he found was a guy — now his partner — and I ended up sandwiched between the two of them."

Raig raised his eyebrows. "Oh, really?"

She went the color of a ripe tomato and put her hands to her cheeks. "Shit, what have I said? Not like that, you idiot." They had both forgotten the interested bystanders.

"Like what?" Raig was all innocence. "I never said a word."

"You didn't need to."

"Er, hello. Earth to you two. Maybe a bit too much info here?" Lorna was waving her hands at them. "I'm still young and innoc— Well, young anyway. I accept it's happened and all that, but I don't want every gory detail."

"Good, you're not getting them," Vairi snapped.

Still not over it then, bless her.

"Probably too much info," Raig agreed, and nudged Vairi. "We'll behave, both of us. Sorry, hon. Anyway, do you want the coffee I said I'd get ages ago?"

"Why not?" Lorna sounded resigned.

Denny gave her a hug. He seemed amused at her discomfiture. "Lorna, love, there's an expression, 'hoist with your own petard', which I think fits this. Let them be. Be glad your mum is who she is. And that Raig has the sense to see it."

"Yeah, I guess." Lorna brightened. "No more show and tell though, okay? That's definitely TMI for me."

"No problem." Raig boiled the kettle, spooned granules into the larger cafetière he'd found and made the coffee as he spoke. He noticed Vairi had disappeared and wondered what she was up to. He didn't have long to wait until he found the answer. Making mischief.

He had poured the screaming liquid out before she returned, his phone in her hand. How the hell had she gotten that? The last he knew, it had been in his pocket.

"It's been vibrating again," she said as she handed it to him with a smirk.

Out of the corner of his eye he saw Lorna and Denny

exchange long-suffering glances. He glanced at the blank screen. "Thanks, love. Nothing to worry about." *Don't overdo it, that's enough for now.*

She must have agreed with him, for she said nothing else, just took her coffee with a smile and moved toward the garden. She threw a pair of maroony-pink flip-flops to Raig, who caught them and put them on his feet, wondering who they belonged to.

"Mine," she murmured. "I read the size wrong." He nodded and carried a tray with the coffee and biscuits out to where a low table and comfortable padded basket chairs waited, the sun warming their cushions, the sound of the bees as they busily moved from flower to bush adding to the lazy somnolence of a sun-kissed morning.

"You know, Mum," Lorna began once they were settled, "this should have been said ages ago, but I am really proud of you. Not many people would survive and thrive like you, or put up with me through my goth and punk years. You never ever screamed or forbade me to have green hair or black nails. So I didn't bother. I had a great childhood and a great role model. Well, maybe not in the 'dancing on a table' scenario, but the rest. I think if I'm being honest, I did sort of suggest to Denny we ask Raig to show you round the fair to get you out of a rut. I should have known you'd embrace that the same way you embrace everything else." She blushed and giggled. "You're right that I was a bit taken aback when, well, when I realized how you'd been entertained, but yeah, I agree, it's not my business."

Denny kissed his wife's cheek. "Way to go, sweet, way to go."

Lorna smiled at him and turned to Raig. "Now's the philosophical bit. All men are hunters. The trouble is that for a lot of them, the thrill is all in the chase. Once they've caught their prey, they either devour it or ignore it. I believe you're one of the good guys, who isn't like that. If I'm wrong, and you hurt my mum, it *will* be my business. I'm a dab hand with the garden shears." She made snipping gestures with two fingers.

He understood the need to protect one's nearest and dearest. Wasn't he just the same? "Point taken. I promise if it is at all in my power, there will be no way I'll hurt her." By omission maybe? He didn't want to think about that.

"Excuse me? Hello? I'm here." Vairi waved at the pair of them. "This is not a hologram. It's a real, live me you can see. With a mind, spirit and voice of my own."

All three turned to her. Embarrassment on Lorna's face, glee on Denny's, and Raig intended love on his.

"Oh, love, no one could ever mistake you for a hologram." He rolled his eyes at her, and she groaned at him.

"The way you said that, Rake O'Shea, did not sound like a compliment."

"It was." He protested, although the amusement in his voice was obvious. "You are much too vibrant, alive, vivacious—"

"Loud?" she interjected in a dangerous tone. He took heed of the warning.

"I never said that, Vairi, my love. Although…" He raised his eyebrows. He remembered very well how loud she could be in certain situations. *So, does she*, he thought, as she glared at him before hastily changing the subject.

"So, Raig, no fair to open today? Sunday a day off?" Denny said loudly, and put his hand over his wife's mouth. "Time to count your takings?"

He smiled. Good, evasive change. "We open at seven for a couple of hours. It's free ticket Sunday. Entry by ticket only. Local schools, kids' clubs and young carers have been given tickets to ride. Wheelchair-friendly ramps to everything, extra helpers, buddies, stuff like that." He had an idea. "Any chance you'd like to help? Any of you? The more the better. We can always do with extra pairs of hands, even if it's just for hugs and handing out the ice creams."

Immediately Raig received three nods and he smiled his approval. "Great. Denny, you and Lorna need to be at the ground by six. Comfy, practical clothes and shoes."

"What about Mum?" Lorna began and giggled self-deprecatingly. "Silly me. Duh, she'll be there, yes?"

Raig wasn't sure that was a question but chose to interpret it as such. "Of course. Ask anyone to show you to the Ready Room if you can't see either of us. Now, are you wanting any more coffee before you go?"

"Raig!" Vairi said with a giggle. "How rude."

"Oh ho, here's your hat. What's the hurry?" That from Lorna.

"Got things to do, eh?" Denny contributed his two pennyworth as all three spoke at once.

"Sorry, and yes." Raig knew he did not sound the least bit repentant, and couldn't care less. He stood up as he eyed a blackbird at the edge of lawn as it waited with patience for any crumbs they might leave. "I've got to go soon, and I need to find my shoes, among other things. Sadly, flip-flops are no good for the site."

"Mmm, dark pink is not really your color, you know," Denny muttered to him as he put his arm around his wife and steered her toward the side of the house.

"Maroon," Raig replied blandly. "Or so I was assured. Shades of red are all the same to me, unless it's shocking pink." He thumped his friend none too gently on his back and kissed Lorna on the cheek. "I'll see you both later."

He watched as Vairi kissed her son-in-law and gave her daughter a hug and a kiss. The love between all of them was obvious. Stupidly, he felt left out, an outsider looking in. It must have showed on his face because Vairi stretched up and kissed his cheek.

"Can't leave you out of my kissing schedule. In fact, you get two." She suited her actions to her words. "And maybe—"

"Too much slush and info going on, Mum. We're off before I blush." With a wave, Lorna and Denny disappeared around the side of the house. Raig waited, holding Vairi's hand before the sound of a car's engine starting up and the change in tempo as it drove off filtered back to them.

"Now then. Where were we before we were so rudely interrupted? Ah yes, I remember." He grabbed hold of a giggling Vairi and put her back into a fireman's lift. "Table or bed?" He was walking toward the door as he spoke.

"The mugs and stuff." She gasped as he ducked her through the low doorway.

Raig glanced down the garden. The speculative blackbird was busy under the table, enjoying its mid-morning snack. Who was he to interrupt him?

"Don't need them. Table or bed?" They were in the kitchen, and he waited to hear her say 'bed'. He was almost at the door to the hallway when she spoke.

"Table. This time."

He spun around. "Table it is. Any ideas how?" He glanced at her face, as she peered up at him with a speculative expression.

"Lots." She was purring. "Oh yes, more than a few. However, this time I'm looking forward to experiencing yours. You know how much time we've got. I'm in your hands."

He swatted her easily reached butt and checked his watch.

"Enough time for starters anyway." Unfortunately, not long enough for everything he'd like to do. Nevertheless, plenty to be going on with.

"So, I'm in charge?" Raig raised one eyebrow. "You'll do as I say?"

She ran her tongue over her lips, an expectant expression on her face and her eyes sparkling with mischief. "As long as it's not illegal, immoral or it makes me fat. Oh, and I can do the 'stop now, it's rotten, I'm calling red thing'. Yeah, I'm in your hands."

He liked the way she described the universal BDSM 'no more, stop immediately' word.

"I promise. I'll do nothing to hurt you or anything you really don't want." He sat her on the edge of the table, so her toes just touched the floor. "*And* I'll honor the 'stop now, it's rotten, I'm calling red thing'."

She giggled. Raig kissed her nose, purely because he loved the way she wriggled it when he stopped.

"Do…not…move. I need to get condoms."

"Third drawer along," Vairi gasped. "In with the serviettes."

Raig looked down at her flushed and sensually charged face. The secret smile playing around her mouth, the way she slipped her tongue between her lips to lick them. He was suddenly parched, needed to drink in her essence, kiss and be kissed.

"My clever Vairi." His voice was husky, as if he was a fifty a day man. "Why the serviette drawer?"

"No one ever uses them. They use paper ones instead."

He could think of a use for them. Several uses. When they had more time. For now, he needed to be inside her. Raig tapped her butt and she lifted up from the table. Within a second he'd moved his hands and lifted her skirt. He gulped, blinked, swallowed and shook his head in pleasure. His cock endeavored to break his jeans zip and the teeth threatened to nip its length if he tried to pull the fastening open.

Shit.

"Hell, love. What a view. What a fucking amazing sight for me to see. Just me, all for me." Again the knickers had been relegated to he knew not, and cared not, where. Her pussy, its nest of curls trimmed oh-so short as to be barely visible, was damp, inviting and ready for him to feast his eyes on.

Soon, I'll get you to dare to go bare, my love.

His body trembled in a delirium of sensations that threatened to swamp him. Raig could truly say he had never felt this depth of emotion before. With utmost tenderness, he stroked his hands up her thighs until he reached the apex and slipped one finger inside her before he flexed his other digits and used them to tease and comb her curls before unerringly finding her clit and massaging it.

Vairi gasped as he varied the strength of his touches.

"Argh, Raig, for fuck's sake, do you know what that does to me? Can you not tell how wet you're making me?"

"Oh yes, and before you come, you'll feel a lot more, I promise." Her pussy clenched his finger as she pulled it in deeper inside her and demanded he show her. Raig obliged with another finger, dancing and playing, scissoring them inside her. His nails gently traced lines on the soft, wet flesh and she groaned deep in her throat.

"M...ore..."

Vairi began to fumble with his zip and a sudden feeling of déjà vu made Raig use one hand to remove hers.

"No. Not this time," he said in a soft tone. "This is for us, in that you come. I stay and watch. Lie down."

"Huh?" Vairi's eyes were cloudy with arousal and she sounded drunk. Gently Raig pushed on her shoulders until her back was flat against the tabletop.

"Lie back, love. Do not move. Please." He opened the ties on the front of her dress that had been beckoning him all morning and revealed her breasts. "Let me show you." Just as he'd thought, she wore no bra, and his eyes were drawn to her tight, hard nipples and the dusky areolae around them. Her breasts were lush and called for his attention, each nub perked and primed for his touch. Raig leaned forward to take both of those tender buds into his mouth in turn. His aim was to increase her arousal to that precious state of pleasure-pain that surrounds the senses. He slipped his spare hand between their bodies again to aid and encourage the one already busy in her pussy and on her clit.

Her juices coated his digits and he knew she was ready to move forward. "Splinter for me, my love. Shatter and come. Show me how I can push you over the edge."

Vairi moaned. Raig increased the tempo, the way his fingers moved and swirled and how his hands touched and caressed. She pulsed hard around him, a gush of liquid covered his hand and she tensed, hard and tight.

She splintered, just as he demanded. Shattered and came

as he requested. Hard and fast. Raig was humbled by such a feeling of love and tenderness and he was hard pressed not to demand if she didn't feel the same.

Not the time.

Vairi shivered and sobbed his name. Shuddered into him, on him and around him. Held on as if he were her only anchor to life and reality. He loved it.

"Ah, love. It's good. Let yourself feel it all. All my love, all for you. That's it. Oh, Vairi My Queen. You are my love."

Chapter Eight

The room was silent except for their harsh breathing. Raig stood in front of Vairi, his hands, unmoving, still on her, his fingers tucked neatly inside her, now at rest. He wondered what she was thinking but didn't choose to break the quietness they were cocooned in. It was a magic moment and he had no intention of breaking the spell before he had to.

Outside a blackbird—the blackbird?—twittered at an unseen annoyance, and Vairi huffed softly. Raig bent his head and kissed her, just above her mons. She stirred and lifted her head. He looked up, his lips hovering just above her skin, taking in the special essence that was Vairi. Strangely, it wasn't the smell of her climax, but the scent of her skin, her hair, her being. He knew, though, that her climax would linger on him long after he had showered. It was part of him.

"What, love?" His tone was tender. "Are you all right? Did I hurt you?"

"No." Her voice was exhausted, as was her face. "No, you never would do that." She fell silent again.

"What then?" Something was wrong, and intuitively he knew she was loath to tell him about it. "Surely it's not so bad that you can't tell me?" He rolled his eyes. "Did you fake it? Is that it? Am I so crap at fingering you, you faked it to get it over and done with?"

That got a response. "Don't be so fucking stupid. You finger fuck like you cock fuck. Exquisitely, erotically and marvelously." She struggled to sit up, clasping him tighter inside as she did. She closed her eyes, but not before he saw what looked like agony in them.

Agony? Shit, what was wrong?

"Vairi. Please, love, tell me." Gently he withdrew his fingers, drew her close and hugged her tightly. "Nothing can be so bad we can't share it. I love you."

"I know." She spoke so quietly he had to strain to hear.

"So?"

"So, that's just it." She leaned her head on his shoulder.

Tenderly Raig pulled her dress together, knowing this was not the time for nudity. He waited patiently for her to continue.

She took a deep, shuddering breath, and didn't look him in the eye. "Raig, you can't. Love me, I mean. Lust for me? Okay, yeah, I'll go with that. Even so, love? You don't know me. I'll accept we are good together sex-wise. More than that? I've no idea. Neither have you, whatever you think. I'm not even sure I believe in love for me. I haven't exactly had much success in that department up to now."

His face felt as if it were carved out of stone. He held himself so rigid every muscle ached. Dammit, he had to try to make her understand his reasoning, his feelings and his determination. There were no two ways about it, no contest, no other ending allowed — they were meant for each other. She *had* to see that. Melodramatic or what? His whole life depended on her doing so, he knew it. Not normally a patient man, for once Raig knew he had to change his reasoning and curb his impatience.

"Oh, my love, and I will not stop calling you that so don't ask. Why not start your success in love by taking a chance on me?" he asked earnestly. "I'll try to be patient. Yes, well" — she was laughing at his words — "I didn't say I'd manage, but I will try. Please, please, *please*, don't give up on us. At least give us a chance. Spend time together, get to know me, learn to love me?" He deliberately put on a hopeful, woeful, puppy dog look. "I'm not a bad guy."

It worked. Sort of.

With a deep sigh, Vairi slowly nodded. "I'll try. At least

I won't bum you off, well, not without due warning. I'm not promising anything though, Raig. You're only here for another week anyway, what then? Text sex? Meetings in a convenient hotel?"

"Now, my Vairi." His heart had lifted somewhat. "There's a thought or two. However, we will sort something positive for us both if that's what we want. We have this week to begin to get to know each other better." He decided not to mention that when the fair left the town, he left the fair to return to…what? Normal life? How the hell did you define 'normal'? His other life?

"So, in the interest of knowing me better, do you want to have your wicked way with me? I'm game if you are?" He raised his eyebrows and did his best to do a sexual leer.

Whether it worked or not, he didn't know. However, Vairi almost giggled and kissed his neck.

"Oh yes. I definitely want to be wicked with you. And some. How much time have we got?"

Raig looked at his watch and turned his wrist to show her. "Probably not enough. Unless you fancy being rapidly wicked?"

Her eyes twinkled at him. "Oh, I can be that." His zip was down and his cock out before he could say a word.

Then he drew a breath, a deep one. Vairi took advantage of it to unbutton his jeans and play with the coarse hair she could now reach and touch with ease.

"Your turn."

"Eh?" Raig had no idea what she meant. His brains were scrambled. "My turn what?"

She moved him so they swapped positions. Took hold of the waistband of his jeans and tugged until they were pooled around his ankles.

"To be on the table." She pinched one butt cheek, making him jump. "Up you go."

It was a no brainer, even if he still had brains to use. Up he went, intrigued to see what she chose to do next.

As he sat on the edge of the tabletop, the wood smooth and

cool against his skin, he thought briefly about splinters and mentally shrugged. If he got any, he hoped she'd be gentle with the tweezers. Raig felt her eyes on him and speculated about what she would do next. Whereas Vairi's feet had dangled, his were flat on the floor. Briefly he imagined how stupid he must look with his jeans around his ankles.

Vairi seemed not to agree as she licked her lips and moved her gaze over him. His mouth suddenly became dry and he unconsciously mimicked her actions and let his tongue run a circle over his increasingly dry lips as she moved toward him and pressed her body close to his. His cock, predictable as ever, rose to the occasion and demanded attention. With a snigger, Vairi obliged and wriggled even closer, until it was held tightly between their bodies. The soft material of her dress cloaked his dick at the same time as questing hands danced over his chest and seconds later his T-shirt was lifted. Eager to accommodate his lover, Raig lifted his arms to assist her and found himself trapped in cloth, arms over his head, face covered.

"Are you claustrophobic?"

Her voice was muffled by the material. Raig shook his head and blew cotton out of his mouth.

"Oh good. Don't move."

The darkness wasn't absolute. He could see outlines and darker areas against the brightness of the day and was able to notice movements and feel her body where it touched him. He stifled a groan as the soft hairs on her arms brushed him and goosebumps broke out to dot his sweat-slicked skin. All his senses were working in overdrive. The ticking of his watch, the beat of his heart, the erotic sighs and catches of her breath, all magnified.

It was his turn to moan, as she took one of his aching nipples into her mouth and nipped and soothed until it was rigid with tension and need. Almost as demanding as his rock-hard cock, which was still trapped between them.

The other nipple received the same attention. Shit, not only did he want to see her with her mouth playing his body so splendidly, he wanted to reciprocate. Raig wasn't used to being passive. Or non-vocal. *Well, Raig, my boy, the times are changing, so change with them. Go with the flow and get the vibes.* He was certainly doing that. Vairi was playing his body, creating new music that sang inside him.

Her naked body — when had she managed that? — rubbed against his heated skin. Cold breath feathered across him, not too cool but to burn. Desperate to hold her against him, he went to move his legs to either side of her and was brought up sharp by strong denim, clamping his legs in one position.

Vairi laughed softly as she tickled his skin. "My show, remember? Stay still, lean back and enjoy."

"Your show, and I can't see the showing," he grumbled, although he knew his voice did not echo the gripe.

"Use your imagination," Vairi advised him. She — well, he hoped to hell it was her and not some random person — lifted his cock and — what? — nestled it between her breasts, her nipples rubbing the skin on either side. Jeez, imagination running in overdrive.

"Fuck, Vairi, yet again you've got me so bloody revved up. I'm gonna come through my imagination *again* at this rate."

"Ooh, good." She was purring. "Although this is nothing imaginary. Can you feel me?" Someone's mouth — *Shit, better pray its hers* — drew his cock in and hot, wet strokes encased its length.

His body arched as if it were on a string, as it strained for more. A press to his chest flattened him back on the tabletop and held him there.

"My show," she reminded him.

Fine. He relaxed as much as it was possible when his cock was being treated to erotic, velvet-smooth strokes inside a wet and tight tunnel, with teeth grazing and teasing its length. He felt nimble fingers on his nipples, holding him down and bringing that overwhelming pleasure-pain at the same time.

All emotions were magnified in his semi-dark, enclosed cocoon, he savored and let himself be overwhelmed. His excitement grew as all he could sense was friction. On his nipples, his cock, his balls. The arousing perception of Vairi's skin moving slightly and arousingly over his. His pre-cum well into her mouth and knew he had to warn her or shoot down her throat.

He didn't get the chance. As he began to spiral out of control, the pressure on his cock increased, the movements faster. Dimly he heard her voice, urging him to let go and come, before those delicious sensations picked up the tempo again. He did as she demanded. Splintered, shattered and came deep inside her.

"Ah shit, Vairi. I'm coming now," Raig shouted even though he understood the warning was too late. It was easy to sense by the way she milked him that she would have done nothing different anyway. Sensations so deep, so heavy, so unlike anything he had ever experienced before bombarded him. He was dizzy, disoriented and unable to form any coherent thought except *yes*. And he reckoned he didn't even have the strength to form the word.

His rapid heartbeat began to slow as his world straightened, even though his cock was still held tight inside Vairi's mouth. No, not tight, just nestled in comfort and love. Or so he wanted to think.

Oh lord, boyo, you have it bad.

Raig had no idea how long they stayed in the same positions, like a tableau, until, his penis flaccid, after one last sensual kiss she slowly moved her mouth away.

Now what? Her hands brushed gently across his chest, and he felt them on his still enveloping T-shirt. The sudden shot of light had him closing his eyes before cautiously opening them again. To the most gorgeous sight imaginable. Vairi naked, tucked between his hardly open legs, holding his jeans around his ankles and pressing her pussy against him. He looked down and laughed. She was standing on a low stool. She followed his gaze and chuckled, sounding self-conscious.

"Well," she said defensively. "It was that, find stilettos, or rub my breasts against your thigh. I preferred the stool and cock approach. The stilettos are upstairs and those balls of yours were calling out for my nipples to touch them. And who am I to ignore the call of the balls?"

His shoulders shook and the laugh bubbling inside him just had to come out.

"Or the call of the wild," he gasped. "Wild and wicked. Bring it all on."

She mock-thumped him.

"Ouch." Raig rubbed his arm as he looked at her. Still naked and himself bare-chested, bare-arsed and his jeans around his ankles it was an erotic sight. He glanced around the sun-filled kitchen with satisfaction.

Sun-filled! His gaze turned to the windows, their curtains clipped back to show a lovely view of… "Oh fuck."

"What?"

He laughed again. "The windows, just as well we've had 'the visit'. We didn't close the curtains."

"Oops. Or lock the door. Oh well, it'd make anyone damn sure never to call unannounced again." She was laughing with him. "Although I'd love to see Stevie's or Lizzie's faces if they caught us in flagrante. Embarrassed but amused."

"They'd know your washing wasn't just up to date and out of the machine. It'd be ironed as well. Or should that be hung out to dry. Ouch." The switch to his leg was feather-light and teasing. "I owe you more than one, Vairi My Queen."

"You'll be hung out to dry if you're not careful, Rake. Watch it."

He grinned.

Vairi stuck out her tongue and rolled her eyes. "If you say 'watch what' or 'I am', I'll scream."

"I won't say either then," he replied promptly. "I'd rather you scream for other reasons."

"Argh." She sniggered as she spoke. "One day I'll have

the last word, Rake O'Shea. Just you wait and see."

"Not today though." He'd noticed the time. "We need to get ready and head to the fair. Ten minutes?"

"Twenty," she said firmly. "If, and only if, I get to shower by myself."

"Spoilsport," he grumbled, not really meaning it.

"Every time," she assured him. "When I am expected to get ready in a hurry. Otherwise I'm a great believer in the beneficial exercise of sport." She reached down to pick her dress off the floor with one hand and gathered up the waistband of his jeans with the other. She slid them up to his knees. "Here, all yours." She looked at the tabletop and patted it. "D'you know something, I'll never be able to drink a glass of milk at this table again." She gave him a kiss, and giggled as she walked to the door. "Oh, and if you want to read the paper it's in the lounge. There's a bit about that reporter bloke I was talking about."

He wondered if he looked as gobsmacked as he felt. As a parting statement, it couldn't be bettered.

"Fifteen minutes," Raig called after her as she left the kitchen, her still-naked butt flashing him a tantalizing farewell. His answer was a wave of the hand.

His jeans zipped but not buttoned, he drank a glass of water — definitely *not* milk — while staring blankly out of the window. How could she behave in such a way with him and not feel more than lust? Ah well, the Chinese water torture was drip, dripping its way into her psyche, he hoped.

He remembered her remark about the newspaper and went to find it.

Shit, shit and double shit. Who had fed the information about another exposé? The article was spare on true facts and high on innuendo, but someone somewhere needed shooting.

"Shower's empty," Vairi called down the stairs.

Pity that. He washed his glass and left it to drain before heading upstairs.

Half an hour later, clean but unfortunately having to wear

the same clothes he had arrived in that morning, he helped her onto the bike, knowing full well the skintight cream trousers and vivid blue shirt she wore like a second skin would be enough to get him hard and the ride would keep him that way. One look at her and he reverted to eighteen and permanently randy. *No, I don't*, he acknowledged as they molded together and flowed around a corner. *I feel* thirty-one *and permanently randy*. He wriggled to try to be seated in a more comfortable position. Behind him, Vairi wriggled too. Accident or design? He didn't deign to guess.

By the time they pulled up at the site entrance, he was more than ready to pull her up. Up and into him. Over and over again. Judging by the look on her face, she felt much the same way.

"Fuck, Raig." She surreptitiously tweaked her jeans as she spoke. "I'll never look at a biker in the same way again."

"Don't look at all unless it's me," Raig advised her with a grin. "As for the rest... I wish, and I want." His look was rueful. "It's going to have to wait though."

"Huh? Oh." She blushed. After all they had experienced together, she still blushed at innuendo face to face. He loved it.

"Come on." He took pity on her and led the way to the compound, where he left his bike. "I need to change."

As she took hold of the hand he held out to her, Vairi nodded toward the paper he had picked up as they'd left the house.

"What do you reckon? He's a star but it must be hard for his family. Never knowing..."

He shrugged. "Someone's in for it. That guy is bullet fodder to a lot of people."

"Well, yeah, I guess. But he does a lot of good, so surely someone will protect him?" Vairi asked. "After all, it's something that needs doing *and* it's bloody good TV."

"Hope so." What else could he say? "Do you think he's right to do what he does even if it puts him and those he loves in danger?"

Vairi tilted her head to one side as she presumably considered his words. "I think I do. If he were my other half, I'd be shit scared every time he went off on assignment or whatever it is, but I'd be proud of him. And you know? Men and women all over the world have jobs that could impact—no, do impact—on their families. That's what keeps our world safe. Why?"

"That's good to know. I, er, just wondered. I do get a bit of aggro in my other job."

She looked at him strangely. "I never knew investment banking was so scary. Never mind, I'll still be on your side."

"Phew, my champion?"

"Yeah, every time."

Now all I have to do is find out how to tell her about my other life and hope she meant it.

They walked across the site, silent and empty except for workers who checked and rechecked safety equipment, rides, stalls, prizes, everything. Some called out greetings, others waved or nodded. Raig felt a visitor-less, deserted, silent fairground during the day was one of the saddest places he ever wandered around. Even the noise of hammers, or people calling to one another, didn't lift the sensation of melancholy. At night, it felt different. Then it was waiting for the next event, any faults and drabness hidden by the all-encompassing cover of darkness and anticipation ran high. In daylight all imperfections were revealed and displayed for all to see.

Raig looked at his empire, all on show, with a critical eye, and was reasonably pleased. Phil was good, better than good even. Raig knew he could leave the following week without any worries. Well, no worries about the fair at least. He'd face the other problem later. First he had his big night out to coordinate and enjoy.

* * * *

"He's a lovely man, you know. Good looking, helpful

and ever so kind. Do anything for any of these charities here." One of the wheelchair pushers spoke to Vairi loud enough for Raig to hear. He doubted Vairi realized that the side of a stall was between them. He'd disappeared to go and sort out a minor problem on a distant booth and been waylaid by several people who'd wanted to thank him for the evening. It had been a good twenty minutes since he'd left her helping entertain the kids in the queue for the chair-o-planes, before he was able to make his way back to her. The evening had gone just as he hoped and there wasn't long left before coaches and cars took the several hundred revelers away and the fairground staff started the big clear up.

"Mmm, I know." Vairi's tone was humorous. Raig grimaced.

"He pays for all this, does Sir Padraig. Out of his own pocket. Mind you, we all know he's as rich as the richest. Sir Paul McCartney's got nothing on him. He doesn't flaunt it or anything. Just helps where and when it's needed. There's a good few kids here with all-singing, all-dancing wheelchairs thanks to him. To say nothing of those adventure holidays for young carers. He's one in a million, is Sir Padraig."

Raig groaned. Shit, shit and double shit. He could imagine Vairi's brain ticking as she homed in on one point the woman had made.

"Er, Sir?" Was that interest or annoyance he could hear?

"Oooh yes." He could tell by the tone of voice the woman was pleased to have someone to pass her knowledge on to. "Not that he uses the Sir bit, you know, being Irish and all that. A bit like Bob Geldof after Live Aid. They get it but can't use it."

She made it sound like a vibrator with no batteries.

"Yes, I see," Vairi said in a noncommittal tone. "Look, it's Benji's turn now." He watched as Vairi helped the boy into the seat and checked he was strapped in safely before she smiled at the helper and walked away. He caught her eye, and she swerved in his direction.

"Well, hello, *Sir* Rake. Do I need to curtsey?" No mistaking the sarcasm. Or the hurt.

"Cut it out, love. I never use it."

"You don't say. Really?" She raised her eyebrows skeptically. "Or choose to mention it either."

He was uncomfortable, just as, he imagined a worm on a hook might feel. "Because it's not important."

Her eyes flashed fire at him. "Not the right answer, Rake. I could have sworn you said I was important. You say you love me, but you don't share something as consequential and relevant as a knighthood. Just because you choose not to use it, do not denigrate it. I don't give a shit about your money. I knew you had to be reasonably well-off from what Lorna and Denny had said, but I don't equate your wealth with you the man. Taking time out to work the fair, owning it. Doing something that could be dangerous. I'm not stupid, there's got to be more than a few quid behind you. But your knighthood? That's an honor. Don't deny something that, whether you like it or not, is such an integral part of you. Not to me, who you profess to love. Some love that. If you lie by omission, how the *hell* can I believe anything you say?" She bit back a sob. "Ah hell, you've made me cry more than anyone in years and I do *not* like it at all. Shit, I told you how I feel about lies. All I ever had from Lorna's dad was lie after lie. I trusted him, and he just about broke me. I swore blind after him that never again was I going to put up with being lied to. By omission or otherwise."

She was struggling not to cry properly, and his heart sank. If she was that upset over his knighthood, what the hell would she say when she found out the rest? He had no illusions it would be 'when' and not 'if'. And it better come from him, not someone else.

"Well, and just how would you like me to bring that into a conversation?" He tamped his rising ire down—anger wouldn't help—and strove to keep his voice level. "And when exactly? Let's screw, and by the way call me Sir when you come? Or, I'm good in bed because I'm a knight? Give me a break here, love. Even to say 'hello, I'm Sir Padraig O'Shea' strikes me as up my own arsiness." He knew his tone of voice made him sound like a sulky kid who'd been caught out doing something wrong, but he couldn't help himself. He might have lied by omission, but he felt what he had said was true. It wasn't something you could drop nonchalantly into a conversation. To be honest, it wasn't something he deemed relevant, or even really thought about. To his mind there were much more important things he had to divulge that were causing him headaches.

He waited. She stared. All around them the noise of the fair continued. Children shrieked and screamed. Generator noises vied with the thumping base coming over the loud speakers. In his mind, all those sounds and people faded to the periphery. Only he and Vairi mattered. He watched the chair-o-plane whirling round above their heads in an absent manner and noticed it was slowing down.

"Isn't there a bit of pot, kettle and black here, Cracking Carry C?" He spoke wearily. "Maybe overreaction? Oh, for f— Heaven's sake, this is neither the time nor the place."

He thought a hint of guilt flashed in her eyes. Perhaps it was pure rage, he had no idea. When she spoke her tone was waspish.

"Again? Oh, how convenient. Shall I make an appointment with your social secretary?" She walked to the ride in preparation to help people off, and he followed her.

"You do that. She's called Vairi McQueen. Ask her when I can speak to you. You know where I am." Sod this, he had work to do. He felt like throwing his hands up in an 'oh, what's the point' gesture, but didn't want to bring any more attention to himself. Few people had noticed the interchange, and that was the way he wanted it to stay. Head held high and smiling at all and sundry, he walked to the Ready Room to collect the goody bags already prepared for each and every child. Over to her now. Yes, he knew he was in the wrong. Yes, he was well aware he was behaving like an ill-mannered brat and yes, he was hurt, angry and fucking scared he'd blown it. And was likely to do so even more in the future. But she'd spat the dummy out as well... hadn't she?

He didn't know if she watched him leave. Tried to tell himself he didn't care. A lie, but one he would try to change into the truth. Hopefully. Eventually. *Fuck it, who the hell do I think I'm kidding here? This is the price I pay for acting like I did. Grow a pair and get over it, for fuck's sake.* Privacy was a wonderful thing, but not when it cost him the one thing that mattered.

There was a tug on his arm and he looked around. A lanky teenager, jeans held up by willpower, was looking at him nervously.

"Mister, er, Sir..."

He smiled and thought of an old song, something about smile, when your heart is breaking. Yup, he could do that. Maybe. "Raig," he said now. "I'm Raig. And you are?"

"Simon Dalton. I'm a carer. I want to say thank you. It's been great. The lady you sent to help Mum is lovely, and she's been a few times to get to know us. She says we're friends now, and she's going to come at least once a week so I can go to extra rugby practice. So, thanks." He held out his hand and Raig shook it.

"My pleasure." He meant it.

The boy turned away, but not before Raig saw the glint of a tear. Compared to what some of these kids had to contend with, his messed-up love life wasn't even a hiccup in the grand scheme of things.

Chapter Nine

He didn't see Vairi again that evening. Apart from a brief text just before midnight stating,

You've fucked up good and proper, you wanker.

He heard nothing from Denny or Lorna either. On automatic, he had spoken to anyone who cared to speak to him, accepting thanks, offering comments and generally not acting like an asshole who had, as Denny so eloquently put it, 'fucked up'. If any of his colleagues noticed her absence, they didn't say, and he managed to get through the chaos of fitting people into the correct buses, tidying up and even locking down the site successfully, all on autopilot. Later, when he looked back, he could remember nothing of the evening after Vairi had walked away.

He didn't join Phil and Jonny for a beer, just spoke a brief, "Stuff to do for work, see you tomorrow," and went back to his trailer, pretending he hadn't heard Jonny's parting shot of, "Get out of your arse, Raig." Trust Jonny.

Easier said than done, he decided as he moodily walked across the scuffed grass. Even the still evening air failed to work its usual magic on him, and instead of expectant, waiting for excitement, the shrouded and shuttered stalls looked sad and lonely. *Just like me*, he thought before mentally kicking himself. *You're a grown man, fucking act like one. You've fucked up. No one else, so it's down to you to sort it. Put up or shut up.*

In a nearby oak tree, an owl hooted, to be answered a few seconds later by its mate. The sound was melancholy and evocative and reminded him of his traveling childhood. *Dusk and time for the creatures of the night,* he mused poetically as he unlocked his trailer, hoping against hope Vairi would be waiting for him. Of course she wasn't. *This is not a bloody fairy story, it's life. No magic wands, no happy-ever-afters unless you make them, mate.*

So he would do that.

Raig took out his laptop and began to send emails. The next stage of his life was hopefully about to begin. An hour later, he was satisfied he'd done as much as he could for a Sunday evening. There were going to be a fair number of people with fireworks under them in the morning, not all of them happy. *So be it.*

Now to start damage limitation. He wouldn't use Vairi's mobile number. Hell, she'd probably refuse to answer his call anyway, besides erasing any texts without reading them. However, he could set the rest of the big grovel rolling. Firstly, with a text to Denny.

Yes, I know, going to try to sort it. Please take care of her for me and ask Lorna not to stalk me with a pair of shears just yet,

His cock shriveled at the idea of Lorna wielding any sort of sharp implement anywhere near his anatomy. She was, he reckoned, not averse to a bit of snip and cut if she deemed it necessary.

Secondly, a quick phone call to a friend with clout in various areas and he was armed with some essential phone numbers. *Not Vairi's landline,* he thought virtuously. To her, he would now behave above board and correctly, including not using her mobile. Even if it killed him.

If she didn't come around fast, it might well end in that.

Raig plotted. It was an uncomfortable position for him to be in, one where he was asking the favors and not the one being asked. For Vairi he would ask — beg if necessary. He prayed it wouldn't be necessary. By the time he fell exhausted into bed, he was as satisfied as he could be that

'Operation Vairi', as he chose to call it, was up and running.

Satisfied, he slept a straight eight hours, to be woken by someone banging on the door. Damn, he felt as if he'd had eight pints and gone ten rounds with Mike Tyson, not two cups of coffee and a full night's sleep. Looking around the bed, the covers neat and scarcely wrinkled, he realized he must have slept like the proverbial log.

"The sleep of the just," he announced smugly to Phil as he pulled open the door to find him on the step, fist poised to thump again. "You want coffee?" He turned and headed for the kettle.

Phil stood in the doorway, staring at him.

"What?' Raig asked quizzically. "What's wrong? I'm zipped and tucked. I need to clean my teeth, have a shower, but as you won't be that close to me, you can cope."

Phil shook his head, his expression bemused. "Are you all right? For someone who was in a dog's mood not ten hours ago, you look awfully happy. Wet dreams?"

"No, you tosser. I slept the sleep of the righteous. Well, newly trying to be righteous at least. I cocked up good and proper, no one but me can un-cock up. Or try to at least. Therefore, I can say with certainty, today is the first day of the rest of my reformed life."

"Uh?"

"I'm a changed man. I'm going to be open and honest and woo Vairi that way."

Phil laughed. "Good luck, mate. I reckon you'll have an uphill struggle. Exactly what does she know?"

He pondered on that for a moment. "She knows my name. My real name. My age. That I own the fair and I'm a Sir. I try to help charities. She assumes I'm an investment banker or something. That's about it, I think."

"Not much then." Phil took the cup proffered.

He didn't know a lot more, and if anything, Raig guessed he probably imagined Raig was only a very part time investment banker and worked as a civil servant and had taken the official secrets act or something.

"Ta." Phil took a sip and grimaced. "Fuck, Raig, no sugar. At eight on a Monday. Come on."

Raig proffered the sugar bowl. *Phil is right*, he decided as he watched the other man add four sugars to his coffee and shuddered at the idea of that sickly sweet taste. He really hadn't told Vairi much. But when had there been time?

"Ye gods, Phil, your heart must be groaning when it discovers how much crap you eat and drink."

"Don't change the subject," Phil told him. "Worry about your heart, not mine."

Just what he intended to do.

"Well then." Phil eyed him edgily. "Are you still finishing your week with us? Or does this mean you'll disappear into your other lives—and no, I don't want the details. Don't know, can't show or sommat—before then?"

Raig shook his head. "I honor my obligations, you sod, you know that."

Phil still looked uncomfortable.

"What? What have I said?" He thought back. "Oh fuck, that came out wrong. I need my time here, Phil. Keeps me sane. Not as an obligation, or to check up on you, shit, you know twice as much as me. No, because for these few weeks I'm just Raig, nothing and no one else."

Phil's face softened. "I'm sorry. I'm being shitty. For fuck's sake, Raig, how the *hell* did you fuck up so spectacularly? One minute you look like you've got the Holy Grail, the next as if someone's cleared out your bank account and pinched your chocolate. You who are usually so on top of things."

"I was on top... Oh fuck... No kiss and tell. Erm." He knew his face was red. Phil was roaring with laughter. Reluctantly he joined in.

"Oh bollocks, I needed that." He wiped his eyes. "If I'm honest, Phil? I'm shit scared. I really have messed up. But, and bear with me here, this is not easy to say, being a so-called macho man and all that, I took one look at Vairi and the caveman took over. Mine, all mine. Sod our ages, sod any baggage, mine. There was enough against me without adding to it. So I kept shtum with regards to quite a lot."

"Yeah, and to be fair, so did she." Phil's voice was even. "Silence isn't always golden, sometimes it's tarnished and dross."

He was quick to jump to Vairi's defense. "Not tight-lipped like me. Okay, I know you don't want all the ins and out of the rest of my life, but some of it is, well, to put it finely, a recipe for a knife in my ribs."

Phil blinked and Raig realized his choice of words could easily be misinterpreted.

"Okay, bastard, you know what I mean. She didn't mention she DJs, but I knew her age, knew she was a commitment-phobe, because she told me. As you said, what did I tell her? Sod all. Well, that's going to change. Everything out in the open and hope to hell she accepts me for what I am. If not?" He shrugged. "Buggered if I know."

He turned away from his friend, not wanting to see the sympathy there. Time to suck it up and get on with it.

"What needs doing?" he asked briskly as he put his phone in his pocket after he'd surreptitiously checked his emails. Nothing. Not that he had expected there to be yet. He ignored the pitying look Phil was giving him. "So?" he prompted. "Anything I need to do? To know? Or do I go back to bed?"

He didn't get there. Nor did he get answers to all his questions. What he did get was an aching back from helping to repair a dodgem and relocate a fruit machine, a headache from banging his skull off said fruit machine, and a heavy heart when his text to Denny asking *Is she still pissed?* came back with a simple *Oh yes.*

Ah well, hopefully later would be better.

It wasn't. The only glimmer of hope was an email saying,

Okay, we'll discuss it when I see you next.

Better than a straightforward no, he supposed. Meanwhile,

he helped out on rides and stalls, fended off a very drunk twenty-something pneumatic blonde who wanted to 'see what it's like with a bit of rough', and broke up a fight between two alcohol-fueled teenagers who both intended to take the same girl on the waltzer. All on a usually quiet Monday night. He wondered if it was something in the water and said as much to Jonny, who smirked and replied, "Vodka."

That gave him his first laugh for a while. He wiped bright red lipstick off one cheek and rubbed the other, where he was fairly sure he'd have a bruise before long. One of the vodka boys had got in a hefty punch before he'd quieted him down.

He sat in his trailer, a beer in his hand, with Phil and Jonny sitting opposite, both cuddling their own bottles, and pondered. Was he doing the right thing? It would mean his life was going to dramatically change, no going back. Was it worth it? Hell yes, no doubts there. Was it going to be easy? Definitely not. In all probability it more likely would cause trouble and repercussions. Then, he was a great believer nothing of any worth was easily gained.

"Earth to Raig. What're you thinking? Hello, we're here."

Oh shit. "Sorry, miles away. Big things on my mind."

Jonny sniggered. "What a thing to say about Vairi, she's only a little thing. Not a big one."

Phil laughed.

Raig managed not to scowl, not to snap, and to keep a bland look on his face by the skin of his teeth.

"Fu-nny," he replied. "Like your face the way it is, do you?"

"Oh, he's got it bad." Jonny looked at Phil, who said nothing, and back to Raig, who knew his poker face was rapidly dissolving into one with more unpleasant emotions showing.

"Fuck, Raig, sorry," Jonny said contritely. "Pretty please leave my baby face the way it is."

Raig smiled, shamefaced, and nodded. "I know I'm like

a kid who's had his computer game smashed, but I'm a bit jittery at the moment." That was the understatement of the century.

"Well, I could say take yourself in hand like a lot of us have to, but don't suppose that's what you want to hear, is it?" Jonny winked. "Not really," he added with a grin.

Raig laughed in spite of himself and shook his head. Hadn't he been thinking he might have to do that very thing?

It wasn't much later before Phil and Jonny left to go to their own trailers. During the days the fair was open, no one was up that long after they had shut down for the night. There was always the knowledge of the work that needed done early the following morning. He checked emails and texts and made sure his plans were taking shape as he wanted and there didn't seem to be any problems before he flopped wearily into bed.

He dreamed. *Vairi sat cross-legged on the bed next to him. Her hair curled around her shoulders and down her back and a long, thin, floaty, multicolored dress covered her from neck to ankles. Her eyes were lackluster and tired, her face sad. 'See what you've done to me? Made me feel like this? You've destroyed my faith, Raig. I liked you, I really liked you. More than I thought possible. The way we could laugh, the way you made me feel when you touched me. I felt special. I even forgot the age difference. I really thought I might just change my mind about love. No need now, I know I was right.'*

'No!' Raig shouted as she got off the bed and walked out. 'No, you're wrong. No. No, please stay…stay… Noooooo.'

He woke up sweating with the word 'no' echoing in his ears and looked at the clock. Half past five. There wasn't a cat in hell's chance he'd get back to sleep now. With a sigh he felt from his head to his toes, Raig decided he might as well get up and go for a run.

An hour later he freely cursed himself. What the hell was he up to? His feet knew exactly where they wanted to go, and like a lovesick fool, he'd let them. To find himself running past Vairi's house and knowing he couldn't stop, open the door, go in and see her was bad enough. But hell, to run past and see a car, not hers, Lorna's or Denny's, was excruciating.

Glutton for punishment, masochist, or both? It served him right, he had no one to blame but himself. The run back seemed to take twice as long and his breath was labored by the time he turned into the site. Unfit? Not really, just uncomfortable with himself. And unhappy. Whose car was at Vairi's? Had they stopped the night? Were they male or female and what relationship did they have with her? None of it his business, all of it eating away at his gut.

A text to Denny —

See anything of Vairi yesterday?

Brought the unsatisfactory answer —

Nah, she was busy last night.

Luckily, he was saved from making a total fool of himself and returning to her house to bang on the door and demand what she was up to, by an email. One that he hurried to answer, and put him in a better frame of mind. It meant he had to give an explanation of sorts to Phil — and intimate he needed to spend the following day taking care of non-fair business. He didn't explain what that business was, and Phil didn't ask. He knew parts of Raig's life and that certain actions and disappearances were not explained until well after the event and sometimes not very satisfactorily, either.

"Going to listen to Midweek Midnight?" Jonny asked him, trying to disguise his interest.

But not very well, Raig thought.

"Pass some time before shut-eye."

"Probably not, too much to do tomorrow. I'd better try and get some sleep." Raig hoped he sounded disinterested. "I'll be back by the time we open, or just after." They were walking back to their trailers after everything had been closed up and had left Phil playing darts with a few of the other men. Raig rubbed his cheek, which, as he'd suspected, did indeed sport a bruise. That was going to go down well. He sighed. Jonny looked at him curiously.

"Second thoughts?" Only Jonny and his parents knew the bulk of his life. Only Jonny knew what he was going to do with the major part of it, after he had cornered him and demanded to know what the hell was going on. Raig admitted to himself that he'd felt a lot happier after he had confided in Jonny, who had agreed he was doing the right thing.

"No," he said now. "Even if it makes no difference to me and Vairi, it's time. Time to move on, either with her, or not. But fuck, Joh, I hope it's with her."

He rocked in his heels as Jonny thumped him none too gently on the shoulder. He grimaced as Jonny laughed and went to move across the grass toward his own trailer. "Listen to the show, Raig," he was advised. "The trailers say it's all about lies and infidelity." With a wave over his shoulder, Jonny left him.

Raig was worried as he unlocked his door. Lies and infidelity. Surely both couldn't be laid at his door? Or was he bumming himself up thinking that nothing involved him and he didn't rate any thought? Strangely, that didn't appeal either. Okay. Then he'd listen. He would *not* admit that nothing could have stopped him.

Checking the time — a quarter to midnight — Raig contemplated the second hand as it swept the face of the clock and decided there was time for a swift shower and something to eat. He put a curry in the microwave before he had the shortest shower known to him.

The microwave bleeped as he re-entered the kitchen and turned the radio and laptop on. No way would he listen and not comment. He had his plot ready. Stage One — Vairi. Retaliation if necessary, wooing if not. He grabbed his curry, put the plate on a tray and settled comfortably on the settee wearing unsnapped jeans and nothing else. Somehow though, when Midweek Midnight was announced, he felt unaccountably worried.

The theme music faded and his cock reacted to Vairi's voice. *Pitiful, Raig, reacting to a voice, for God's sake.* But there it was, visible for him to see. A positive reaction. He sat, resigned, ready, no, not ready, but in a fatalistic mood to listen to himself being crucified. As the music faded, he became aware he was leaning forward, waiting to hear what she said.

"Midnight people, welcome." The voice was mellifluous and as ever Raig's cock, already hard, responded to the tone and hit his jeans as it demanded release. *Ah, fuck, down boy. For now, listen and learn.*

"So, people, lots to discuss tonight. But first, *I Will Survive* by Gloria Gaynor."

Oh shit, shit and double shit. It was going to be nasty, he just knew it.

The music faded, and that beloved voice spoke again.

"Now, midnight people, what are your thoughts on lies and infidelity? Any excuses for either? Let me know? You have the address. Email your thoughts. While you do, let's listen to *Sorry Seems to be the Hardest Word* by Elton John. You know, for most of the assholes in this world that is oh-so-very true."

Yup, she'd got that spot-on all right. How the hell was he going to address that? *Man up and go for it.* He wrote an email rapidly, checked the spelling—he'd be damned if he'd get mocked for that as well as everything else—considered it, decided it would do and pressed send. Then, nerves in a knot, Raig waited.

He was not disappointed. The song faded and Vairi's voice replaced it.

"Well, peeps, comments already. Raig says sometimes it happens. Hello, Raig. Why? Lies are so not acceptable, you tell me why you think they are. Micky D says what is infidelity. Okay, folks, let me tell you. It is when someone lies. Does not tell the truth. For me it is not cheating with sex. It is cheating with the truth. What do you say? How should you answer? Let us know."

Oh, he would.

Ninety minutes and several emails later, he was angry. Angry and frustrated. After those first two emails and replies, his comments were ignored apart from a brief, "Lots of comments from the same person tonight. Guilty conscience, do we think?"

Well, yes, of course it was. He knew that. She knew that. Fuck, by now several thousand listeners knew that. His next email did get read out.

"Now, midnight people. What have we here? A groveling email." He could hear the glee in her voice. "One I must share with you. It's not often we get something like this. First let's have some appropriate music. I was trying to find something with 'yes, I am a prick' in it, but hey ho, neither Stevie, Andie nor I could manage that. So we've come up with David Gray." The words from his song *Babylon*, which presumably explained what she meant, came out of the speaker.

Raig grinned. Did she understand he knew he might be acting strangely and wanted her to forgive him? Firstly, though, he was going to have his heart laid bare over the airwaves.

The music faded. "So, folks, here's the email I was talking about. Unusually, I'm not going to give you this person's name. The email wasn't sent in anonymously, but we feel this person deserves not to be totally lambasted. Well, Stevie does anyway. I'm not so sure."

Not forgiven then.

"I'm going to call this person 'he', but it may be a man or a woman. We're not saying. Here goes." He could imagine her take a deep breath. In effect she was showing everyone how he felt about her.

"Carry C, I've cocked up big time. I've met someone who I fell for, deeply and truly. This person is all I ever want, they make my life complete." She broke off and cleared her throat. "We're paraphrasing a bit here, peeps. Bear with us. Where was I? Ah, yes, this person makes my life complete. The problem is I didn't mention something about me and my life. Well, more than one something actually. To me, part of what I didn't say doesn't seem important. To this person, it meant I was lying by omission. And I was, wasn't I? Even if I didn't realize it. She—remember it could really be he—won't speak to me. I think she won't anyway. I have her mobile number but don't think I should phone. Not yet. To be honest, I'm scared to in case she either doesn't answer or cuts the call. She's been lied to big-time before and won't stand for it. Neither should she. I was wrong, and I admit it. Although, she wasn't totally snow white in all this and didn't mention her job to me. That I found out, by default. Please, Carry C, if she hears this, tell her I love her. I'm so sorry I was an idiot. Can you ask her to give me another chance? The only thing is, I do have another part of my life I can't discuss yet. I'm not married, I'm not a spy or a criminal, and I'm not insolvent, but somethings can't be shared until I'm allowed to. Oh god, that sounds overdramatic, but it's true. Yes, it does, doesn't it?" Vairi said huskily. "Hmm, now let me get this finished. So this person goes on to say, 'Hopefully very soon, I'll be able to tell her everything about me. Share all of me with all of her. I believe in fidelity, truth and honesty. I'll give her all of that and more if she'll let me. Do you think I have a chance?'"

Chapter Ten

There was silence from the radio. Raig held his breath as he waited for Vairi to comment again.

"Well, peeps, what can I say?" She sounded breathless. "What an admission. What do I say to that? Here's Cliff Richard and *Miss You Nights*."

Raig felt like he was in a time warp. Where did she find them? What next, Perry Como and *Magic Moments*? There was a thought. He decided she needed another email. Hopefully one she'd laugh at.

She did. As the song ended, he heard her laughing. "Welcome back. I've had a very nice email from a listener. He wants Rod Stewart singing *Da Ya Think I'm Sexy?* for his lovely lady. So here it is. Then we'll check out some more emails. I must say our mystery person has got a lot of sympathy from you. Even from those of you who say he was in the wrong."

His laptop beeped to indicate an incoming email. Brief. To the point.

Sexy. But still a wanker.

Aha. Presumably Stevie was seeing the emails. He checked again and felt he'd won the lottery. Across the bottom it stated, *sent from my iPhone.*

So, no Stevie to read and comment, that was a step forward. She hadn't suggested she play *Return to Sender* either.

This sexy wanker really is sorry. He admits he still hasn't told

131

the truth, the whole truth, and nothing but the truth, but he is working on it. Hopes to be working on you one day!

Too much? He still pressed send.

The rest of her show passed uneventfully. He received no more emails and wondered if he had been too blatant.

Just as he went to log off, he heard the familiar bleep. Twice. One said, *read first.*

He opened it.

A work in progress? Let me know when you've finished.

Oh, he'd do that all right. He opened the second one.

Should I be flattered? Or annoyed? Guess I'll think about that and let you know. Meanwhile sleep well. Sweet dreams!

Not much chance of that. Even those few words had raised his hope. And his cock.

In a considerably better frame of mind, he went to bed. Frustrated and horny as he was, he had no intention of doing anything about it. That *would* be infidelity. He kept his hands strictly at his sides and woke up feeling better than he had in days. He even whistled as he got ready to head for the first of several of what he thought would be difficult meetings. He wasn't wrong. His ideas were argued against. Everything he suggested was counter suggested. Vehemently.

"Look, Raig, I can see where you are coming from, but it's your life at risk here. That heroin gang meant what they said, you know. Michael Dooley is a dead man. He's a dead man walking, that's there very words. You can't risk it. No way. If it's not them, it will be someone else."

Raig was stubborn and determined — it was his future at stake. "There has got to be a way. We need to find it and make it work. I was out of it soon anyway. I need to make it official. Finished. You might have been hoping I'd sign on for another stint, but I told you, you know, Kenny. Enough is enough. Next week is it. One way or another."

The man sighed and ran his hands over his sparse hair. Hair that, he joked, had been thick, dark and luxurious until he'd met Raig. "Okay. Let's see what we can do. I still think you may need to be ultra-cautious though. No exposé, just a getaway."

Raig grunted. He'd guessed that already. It was how it would be done, that was the important thing. Already he had managed to bring the meeting forward. Now he just had to bring the demise of Michael Dooley forward as well.

"It matters," he said now. "More than anything has ever mattered. Even more than all this." He waved his hands around the tiny room. "She is my life, I hope. She's everything to me." Trite but true. "My da always said I would see her and know. And I have. We've got to get this right, Kenny. Too much is at stake."

"You're telling me, but somehow I don't think we are talking about the same things."

"Probably not," Raig acknowledged. "Nonetheless, both are very important. Right, so I can leave it up to you for now? I'll be back on Monday."

Kenny nodded, his eyes grave. Raig felt a moment's pity. He'd blithely said what he wanted and was leaving it up to Kenny to make sure it happened. Raig touched his shoulder.

"Thanks," he said simply. "It will all be worth it, I promise. I won't do anything stupid, will do as I'm told, but even so, for my sanity and future, it's got to be over."

"I know. I'll get things rolling. We'll go for Thursday next week, as arranged."

Raig smiled as he left the room, his heart heavy, where it should have been light. Nevertheless, no one understood more than him just how much he was risking. Half of him wished it could be over and done with sooner, the other half knew how important it was to get it right.

As he drove back to the fairground, he went over everything in his mind. He was going to have to make sure Vairi understood it all. That might prove tricky. He had to ask her to wait for another week before he revealed everything, before he was up front with her. Would she do that? He needed help. Jonny. He was the only person, other than Kenny and his helper, who knew exactly what he had been doing. Who Michael Dooley was, and what he was to Raig.

So tonight after close-down, he'd enlist Jonny.

"You're fucking mad. Absolutely off your trolley. Deathwish dot com, that's you. Crazy, fucking crazy." Jonny threw his hands up in disgust. "Ninety pence short of a quid. Hello, I like having you around. Your ma will kill me if I tell her I'm about to arrange your funeral. It's impossible."

"Not if it's done properly," Raig argued. "I need you to help me, Joh. If I give you what and where, I need your help. No one else can do it. There's no one else I trust."

He thought, hoped, he had mollified Jonny. It was true. Only he could help now.

Jonny sighed deeply and nodded. "I'll help," he said gruffly. "But for fuck's sake."

"Be careful," they said together.

"Oh, fuck you, Raig. Just please, please do as you're told. Seriously, your ma would never forgive me if it all goes tits up."

Raig laughed. "Never mind Ma, I wouldn't forgive myself. Right, I'm for bed. I've a lot to do in the next few days, not just here. Thanks, Joh. I owe you."

Jonny grimaced. "That you do, Raig, that you do. I'll remember."

Raig laughed. "I bet you will, you bugger."

Jonny's promise of help gave him the fillip he needed. He slept well and woke up on Friday morning ready for anything life threw at him. So he thought.

His determination was tested almost as soon as he got up and went to the Ready Room. Phil had a face like a wet week in June.

"What's up?"

Phil scowled. "Half the fucking stallholders, that's what. Bloody throwing up. D and V courtesy of Tessa Willows and her bloody mushroom soup. Magic bloody mushrooms. We've got environmental health all over us like a rash."

In spite of the fact that it seemed like half of the stalls wouldn't be able to open, Raig couldn't help but laugh. Tessa was famous for adding something extra into her cooking. Her devotees had got more than they'd bargained for this time. Unfortunately, however bad their resultant headaches might eventually be, the one Phil had now was much, much worse.

"So, worst-case scenario, Phil?" His own problems would need to wait. "What are we down?"

"Anything from ten to twenty won't be fit tonight. Tessa is being the original weeping willow and fucking useless. Typical though, she's fine of course. Never hits the one who causes it, eh? We can cover about half the rides, but" — he shrugged — "let's hope it's a quiet night."

"Not likely on a Friday. I'll see what I can do to get help. Give me a while." He walked away from Phil, who was already muttering and cross-referencing people to stalls and rides, and pulled out his mobile. Okay. Denny would be working, but that had never stopped him answering his phone before. God willing, it wouldn't this time. It didn't.

"Hey you. How's the dick?"

Nice greeting that. Expected, but nevertheless…

"Still attached. Look, Denny, we need help. Not me, the fair." Briefly, he explained about the dodgy food.

He heard the interest in Denny's voice as Denny chuckled and asked teasingly, "What sort of help do you need?"

Rapidly, Raig went over what he thought they needed. "I know I can't use anyone to man the rides, because of health and safety, but as general dogsbodies, that sort of thing would be a great help. Hell, anyone who can string three words together and speak intelligibly will do. Oh, and they need to promise not to eat anything that Tessa Willows offers them. She seems to have a cast-iron stomach, nothing affects her, but by God, her cooking can't half affect others. We're in a real hole at the moment, Den. We've only got another three nights here, I really don't want to have to close half of the attractions for one of them."

"I'll see what I can do. What time?"

Within seconds Raig put down the phone. He'd done all he could. Now he had to wait and see how things panned out.

Phil looked harassed as he re-entered the Ready Room. "Bloody Tessa. Why does she never experience the results of her handiwork? That's another two feeling queasy. Although to be fair with these two, it could be cider and not soup."

Raig shut the door behind him and put the kettle on to make a large pot of coffee. "I've asked Denny if he can sort any helpers for us because he's got the rugby club to call on. They can do all the grunt work and let the professionals cover the rest. I've given him your mobile number." He leaned against the work surface until the kettle began to whistle, then busied himself with making the brew.

"All we can do for now, I guess." Phil took the proffered cup with a word of gratitude. Raig looked at him, thankful for such a good manager. He was even *more* thankful he was not the one to sort all the problems out.

"We're lucky it's only Tessa and her soup that's the problem, or we would be in big trouble," Phil continued. "As it is, I contacted the authorities when I heard, and we're on top of it. We can't open any food stalls, but the rides and sideshows are good to go, if we have enough bodies to man them. Or woman them, no sexism allowed here." He smiled briefly, although Raig noticed it hardly reached his eyes. Phil was tired, irritable and rightly fed up. "Bloody Tessa. She's a liability, Raig. This is costing us, big time."

He nodded. "You're the boss. If you feel we can't use her any more, over to you. Fortune-tellers are ten a penny. Actually, no, they aren't, but still, no one is irreplaceable. I wonder if she read all the trouble she's caused in her tea leaves? If she's as good as she says she is, she bloody well should have. Anyway, up to you."

"Thanks a lot, boss! I'll let you know." Phil sounded resigned.

Raig nodded. Boss in name only. Phil well knew all fair hiring and firing was up to himself. Raig was definitely the sleeping partner. The man with the money. The way he liked it. Now he needed to go and earn some of that money.

"I've an appointment with my computer." He finished his own coffee and set down his cup. "I'll keep my phone on, so you can disturb me if you need to. I mean it, Phil, today, you can disturb me, it's fine."

"Cheers, now bugger off and let me worry in peace."

He laughed, and with a brief wave, did as he was told. However, once back in his trailer, he couldn't settle to anything. His mind kept returning to Vairi and that email. Did it really mean anything, or was he reading things into it that weren't there? One way to find out.

Slept like the proverbial log!

Would she get the innuendo?

Very stiff when I woke up. How about you?

He found the right email address and pressed send. Nothing else to do, except wait, get on with his own work and try to forget everything else. To his astonishment, he did just that and an hour or so later registered the fact he had earned a considerable sum of money. Wheeling and dealing got his adrenaline going and made his bank manger happy, that was for sure. If only he could deal with the rest of his life as satisfactorily.

His personal inbox remained stubbornly empty no matter how often he refreshed it—a good sign or a bad one, he had no idea. Resigned, he resolutely turned to the next work matter on his mental agenda. The demise of Michael Dooley. Truth be told, he was sick of him, the way he had infiltrated his life and tried to take over was scary, especially with the underlying threats involved. He would be more than glad when he no longer existed.

Diligently he planned and plotted, and when he was satisfied, he emailed his suggestions to Kenny. Waited again. Something he was not very good at doing. To help pass the time, he stripped and remade his bed, reluctantly losing the faint scent of Vairi that had been sustaining him. *Onward and upward, Raig*, he told himself as he put the bedding in the washing machine, added powder and switched it on. *You don't need the scent of her to remember everything.* His cock twitched as if to agree with him. He glanced wryly in its direction. *Down boy. I didn't mean that sort of upward.* Not the state to be in at the moment, but it was easier said than done.

The beep of his laptop took him by surprise. He was taken aback by his disinclination to look and see who it was from, in case he was disappointed. Before he had walked to where he had left it on the table, it beeped twice more. He took a deep breath and opening up his emails, checked his inbox.

Kenny, Kenny, and — oh thank you, gods — Vairi. He opened that one first. Sod the 'waiting is good for you' diktat. Not at the moment it wasn't.

I don't get hard. I do get even. Ache and learn. P.S. Wet here.

The laugh that erupted took him by surprise. Clever Vairi, it was brilliant sunshine, wall-to-wall blue sky and warm. No precipitation anywhere.

It could get wet here with a little help. Any takers?

He pressed send and wondered if she would reply. She did, and remarkably quickly.

No. Ache and learn. See you later.

Did that mean what he hoped it did? Would she be one of

Denny's helpers? Ache indeed. His whole body throbbed with need.

The other two emails were more complicated, and he had to think long and hard before he answered them. In the end, he reluctantly agreed to Kenny's demands, knowing realistically what he suggested — demanded — was the only way to go. His stomach rumbled, and he realized with a jolt he hadn't eaten anything all day. It was now or probably never.

He took a lasagna out of the freezer, and with a brief prayer of thanks to his ma for all her cooking and baking, Raig popped it in the microwave.

He had just finished eating when his phone rang. He checked the caller. Phil.

"Hi, what's up?" Even though he had told Phil he could contact him for anything, it was not like him to take him up on his word.

"Not a lot really." Phil sounded upbeat. "Denny has organized well over a dozen helpers, including a D.J." He chuckled, knowing the inference Raig would take from his last words. Vairi was one of those co-opted for the evening. "Three mushroom morons are okay to work, and a couple more will be fine to man the phones and the ticket booth. As we can't have the fast food stalls or candy floss open, we should just about scrape through. I'll know more nearer six. You okay to be here by then?"

He answered with more composure than he thought possible. "No problem. I'll see you in a bit."

Would Vairi be there? He could only hope.

The Ready Room was crowded by the time Raig squeezed in. A last-minute phone call from Kenny had held up his arrival. A well worthwhile hold up — his plans were progressing better than he could have imagined and there were just four more days to go before they were able to start putting them into practice. In a week, it would all be over.

Raig scanned the room and added his thanks to Phil's telling everyone how relieved he was they had offered to help. "I'm leaving the what you do to Phil. He tells me what to do — and often where to go," he added as there was spontaneous laughter. "We really do appreciate you helping us like this. Just don't eat anything Tessa, our fortune teller, offers you. Great fortune teller, as long as it doesn't involve her, but a terrible cook. To say she takes creativity to its limits is an understatement." Stepping back, he leaned against the wall, deflated he could see no Vairi, before spotting her tucked in behind a big, burly rugby player type.

Phil began placing people to jobs. Raig, watching them leave, half listened, more intent on observing Vairi. She looked tired, dark shadows under her eyes, a droop to her luscious mouth.

"Raig, you take the gallopers with Vairi. Okay, Vairi?"

She nodded. Didn't look at Raig.

He looked at her though and drank in the view. Her long, dark hair was tied back into an intricate braid, her breasts confined under a bright pink T-shirt that hurt the eyes but drew them back. Her long, shapely legs, encased in dark denim, ended in those hard-on-inducing, sparkly flats, all designed, he was sure, to make him want to take every last piece off her. His cock, having behaved up to then, immediately changed its mind about the state it was in.

He watched her eyes drift down and widen slightly before returning to his face. Although she made no comment, he heard her breath quicken. Not unaffected, thank goodness.

"Come on then, Vairi My Queen," he said cheerfully, not bothering to either hide or quell his reaction to her. "Let's hit the horses."

She winced.

"You'll not be on them. I need you to man, oops, *woman* the gates for me."

She nodded and let him usher her out of the room. He saw Phil's grin. Matchmaker, mischief-maker, or meddler? What's in a name?

"I'm still pissed," was the first thing she said to him as

they made their way over the well-trodden grass, the noise of the generators beginning to fill the air.

He nodded. "Guessed you would be. I appreciate your help."

Her eyes were everywhere except on him. Patiently, he waited to see if she would add anything else.

"This doesn't mean I forgive you, you asshole." Her voice would cut ice. "I'm here because Denny asked me, and here with you because Phil said. No other reason."

Raig kept his face straight with difficulty. Who was spitting the dummy out now? He decided discretion was the way to go and chose not to mention that.

"We both appreciate it, Vairi," Raig said, sincerely. "Especially as it must have gone against your principles to help the baddy." He winked. "Who honestly isn't rotten right to the core."

A slow grin spread over her face and she laughed, reluctantly. "Oh, shut it, you moron. I'm still not playing. I didn't bring my ball."

"No problem, I've got two we can share." Raig winked and mock-winced as she punched his shoulder. God, how easy it was to slip back into their bantering.

"Hmm, I don't share. Ever."

"Neither do I, Vairi My Queen. Neither do I. Right, let's away to the gallopers. I promise you won't need to move around on the ride." He held out his hand. She looked at it then at his face. He could see the indecision on her eyes before, reluctantly, she nodded and took hold of it.

"For the record, I'm staying pissed with you," Vairi informed him as he unlocked the gate in the security fence around the galloping horses. "I've decided I don't get mad often enough. I enjoy a good mad if it's needed." She stopped and looked at him. "This was needed."

"I accept that. However, for the record, I still have secrets I can't let you in on yet," Raig replied. "I hope when I do, you'll stop being pissed." Oh, how he hoped.

"Hmm. So, when do you own up and spill the beans?"

Vairi's voice was that of a child lost in an adult's world and who wasn't happy.

"Soon. Maybe in a week if all goes well." He snuck a quick kiss.

She glared at him. He thought she might just stamp her foot. "Why not now?"

"I can't. When you do hear what I have to say, I hope you'll understand." If not? Well, if not, there was nothing more he could do. He would have to accept that was it. Finished. "I know it's a lot to ask, but I need you to trust me on this one, love." Her expression hadn't changed. "Vairi, don't tell me not to call you love. Because I won't stop. You. Are. My. Love. Get used it."

Chapter Eleven

She glowered.

Raig grinned as he ushered her through the gates of the perimeter fence around the galloping horses. "Next Thursday you'll know everything, on my oath. Keep the night free. In fact, keep Friday free. We've a lot to catch up on. It won't be *Saturday Night's Alright for Fighting*. It'll be Friday day and night are fine for fucking."

This time her laughter was unforced. "Only fine? You disappoint me."

Raig grinned. "It scanned better than bloody marvelous, brilliant and amazing." He covered all the safety checks, signed them off in the book and explained to Vairi what she had to do.

"Basically, you're the policeman, or the lollipop lady. Wait till everyone is off before letting anyone on, and count to make sure everyone can get a ride. Don't be afraid to shut the gate while you check. There're fifty-four horses on it. Although some people will double up." He didn't add, 'like we did', but her eyes glazed and again her breath quickened.

"We're doing tickets only today, so they need to go to a booth first."

She nodded her understanding. He felt her eyes on him as he moved to the mechanism and set the ride going, Rod Stewart blaring out *Da Ya Think I'm Sexy?* from the speakers.

As he looked toward her, he could have sworn after her initial laugh, she blanched as the thing went around. With luck, she was remembering her motion sickness, and it wasn't the song, or worse, the climax she'd experienced, that made her look so pale.

Nimbly he leaped onto the moving floor, walked over and jumped off near to where she was standing. Already the first few visitors were trickling up. Less chance of a slapped face if he kissed her? Raig decided it was worth a try, and while she didn't reciprocate, she didn't pull away either. Hopefully it was a good sign. He ignored the muttered, "Fucking chancer." There didn't seem to be any heat in her words and she wasn't glaring at him.

"Okay, love, are you ready once I stop it?" He smiled cheekily as he spoke.

Vairi harrumphed. "As ready as I can be."

"Good show. Look, Vairi, on a serious note, I really appreciate you coming along tonight. I hoped you would but wouldn't have blamed you if you didn't. I was a plonker."

She nodded. "Oh, yes. You can say that again."

"Ah no, I can't. Once is enough."

Vairi rolled her eyes. "I'm taking the fifth on that. So what else do I need to know?"

Raig ran over the instructions she'd need in his mind. "Wave or use the radio if you need help. I'll be in the middle on that high step, and I'll keep looking over. Don't open the gates till I've bought it to a stop this time. Every other time, don't open them till it's empty. The gates are marked *Entry* and *Exit* and I'll get to the exit to stop chancers trying to get in that way. There's not enough bodies to have someone else there. Right, give me a minute to slow it to a stop. When it's full, use the radio to tell me. 'Kay?"

Vairi nodded. "Bring 'em on."

Raig kissed her again as the urge to pull her tight and grind her against his hardening cock was almost irresistible. It took more strength of mind than he'd known he possessed around her to resist and get himself to where he needed to be. *Concentrate on your work, not your gonads, man.*

The next couple of hours were hectic, and Raig had no problem ignoring his body. He kept an eye on her as she saw people on and off the carousel and occasionally heard the banter and chat she carried on. Kids shrieked, teens chattered and squealed and over it all the tinny fairground music blared out. Raig worked on automatic as he manned the ride, kept an eye out for fights and sorted a few youths out who thought they'd have a free ride and tried to hop the fence.

As the evening progressed, he wondered why he could feel nothing except pleasant friendship for most people, but then, wham, one person hit him like a ton of bricks and brought out every protective, loving, chauvinistic, caveman feeling he possessed.

Every smile Vairi threw at a male of any age made him want to snarl. Put a sign on her saying, *Hands off, she's mine.* Throw her over his shoulder and lock her out of sight. *Get a grip,* he told himself in disgust. It was so unfunny, it was laughable. He had it bad.

Every so often he caught Vairi looking at him, in that 'come and take me, I'm yours' way she had. Raig decided she didn't even know she did it and would no doubt be mortified if he told her. So he absorbed and enjoyed the heat it sent through his body.

After a couple of hours, he made his swaying way over to her. He could have easily used the radio but enjoyed the look of 'oh my God, macho man antics' she threw at him as he jumped on and off the moving roundabout.

"No more after these get on. We're going to be relieved by Phil and someone so we can have a quickie break." He misused the word intentionally.

She giggled. "In your dreams, carnie-man. I need food. And a coffee." She paused, and he wondered what she was going to say. His cock thickened and hardened from the semi-erect state it always seemed to be in when she was near, to the zip-breaking one it preferred around her. *A bloody efficient Vairi-alert!*

"As I'm in a good mood, as a gesture, I'll spend my break with you." She patted his cheek. "To make you wish and writhe."

She did that all right. After ten minutes of watching her practically make love to the baguette he'd filled with chicken salad for her in his trailer, and continuing the visual eroticism and teasing with an ice-lolly, his cock was so hard he could have used it to break ice. *Or the bloody ice-lolly. Kung Fu Cock!*

The idea made his lips twitch.

"What?" Vairi must have noticed the smirk.

Should he tell her? Hell, why not, she seemed to have melted slightly toward him. A bit like that sodding ice-lolly, which was rapidly staining her lips the color of her other lips.

"You've made me so fucking hard, my cock could cut that lolly in half. I was thinking it was going to take up martial arts."

She got the inference. "Oh well, be my guest, feel free." Slowly with a little plop, the remains of the ice-pole slipped from her lips and, with a swipe of her tongue over her mouth, Vairi held it toward him. Wickedly, Raig moved his hands to his zip, and very slowly lowered it an inch. Her eyes widened. He stopped, and left that tantalizing opening to tease and, with luck, draw her eyes.

"Nah," he drawled, bringing her gaze back to his face from the quick glance she had indeed flicked toward his zip. "Too easy. You've fucked most of it away." Her eyes widened at his crudity, but she didn't comment on it.

He watched her shrug. "Oh well, I'll finish it off myself."

Yeah, no doubt. It was a pity it didn't happen to be his incipient climax she was talking about. Did she have *any* idea what she was doing to him? Of course she did, that wicked glint told him just how much she was enjoying herself. Raig surreptitiously adjusted himself as he stood and threw his cold coffee down the sink. "Ready to get back? You don't have to if you don't want to. You've done a lot already, and boy is it all appreciated."

"All?"

The remains of the slippery lolly disappeared down her throat, and she wiped her hands and lips on a paper napkin. It reminded him of her serviette drawer, and he mentally groaned.

"Oh, good." She added and touched her upper lip with the tip of her tongue.

His hard-on, which he had been doing his best to control and make become a semi-hard-on, immediately changed tracks and roared back into violent action. She noticed, damn it. It would be hard — he groaned, *don't use that word even in your mind,* he admonished himself — not to, the zip on his denims almost unzipping itself. Raig decided to be blatant about it.

"This" — he gestured toward his cock — "is due to you. Your name, your voice, thinking of you, and I'm hard. I literally ache for you, Vairi My Queen. I dream you are with me, and I'm touching you, absorbing those arousing love sounds you make, feeling you touching me. I wake up rock-hard and realize you aren't with me. A sobering thought when I know, even when I am able to open up, you still might not want me, trust me."

Her face was clouded as he gently touched her cheeks and kissed her. "Don't worry, my love. I'm telling you because I promised I would be as open and honest as I could at any time. I'm not asking you to comment, make a commitment, or anything. Just to listen and hold the thought. Will you do that?"

Vairi nodded.

"Thank the gods." He kissed her again. Hard, but lighthearted. "Right, shall we go?" Raig locked the door before he took her hand and they walked back across the site toward the carousel. As usual, the sights and sounds of his beloved fair raised his spirits.

"Hell, I *love* this. The sounds and smells of my childhood. The scratchy music either one notch too soft, so you can't catch all of it, or one too loud, so you're bombarded. Diesel and usually grease from chips and popcorn. Huh, I can feel that missing. It's as if only half of everything is alive. Grease apart, the crying kids, screaming teens and squawking parents and oldies? I love it all!"

Vairi laughed. "Easily pleased, then?"

"Oh, love," he all but purred, "so very easy, you wouldn't imagine. Hopefully though, I'll soon be showing you." They had reached the barriers by the carousel and received some resentful looks as with a polite "excuse me", he escorted Vairi to the exit gate.

Before he had a chance to key in the password to allow them through, someone challenged him. "Oy, mate, there's a bloody queue here for a reason, you know." The speaker, twenty-something, tattooed and belligerent, was glaring at him from the snaking line of people He was holding the hand of a tiny girl dressed in a tiara, bright pink frilly jumper and reach-for-the-sunglasses shocking orange and purple leggings, who met the 'you must be this tall to ride' level by a centimeter. "Dubonnet-Auriel has been waiting ages."

What the…? He saw Vairi turn away and had to stifle his own grin. Which soap did that mouthful come from?

"Of course, sir," he said smoothly. "However, if we don't come through, there won't be a ride. We've just had our mandatory break and are returning to run the ride for you. The staff there at the moment need to take their break. We are most careful to ensure everything is done to achieve your safely and enjoyment." Shit, he sounded like a pompous old git. Nevertheless, the words seemed to mollify the man, who nodded.

"Berra get on then, eh. Or I'll not be best pleased."

It was Raig's turn to nod as he waited for Vairi to enter the compound and shut the gate behind them. Her lips twitched, but wisely she faced away from the queue.

"Why not call her Tia Maria or Whisky Tango?" she muttered.

"Already taken, by some drinks company and the police. If I was being non-PC, the latter is where he looks as if he is heading. As I'm not I'll just say, see you in a mo," he muttered out of the side of his mouth, before smiling at the girl waiting for Vairi to relieve her. In one smooth leap he vaulted onto the ride, crossed the floor between the rising and falling horses and reached the middle so he could jump down and stand next to Phil, who was about to stop the roundabout.

Phil nodded toward Vairi. "All back on track?"

"I wish! Still, she's talking to me, so that's a positive." Even Phil didn't know everything about his life, so he probably thought Vairi was overreacting. However, he merely nodded before handing the keys over to Raig, who signed for then with an unintelligible scribble and his name printed afterward. "Cheers, Phil. Closing at eleven?"

"Yup, and I'll tell you for nothing, I'll be more than pleased when we get there."

So would Raig, except it meant the last he would see of Vairi for a while. Time to enjoy being with her while he could.

As the last ride slowed, stopped, and the final stragglers moved away, Raig went across to where Vairi stood waiting for him.

"Want a ride?" His tone was bland, the innuendo clear.

Laughing, she shook her head.

"On that?" She pointed to the unmoving roundabout. "No way. On you, ditto. You want a ride, you go on it. Ride the horsey, cowboy. Show me how it's done." Her innuendo was equally as clear—her assumption he would blow her request off showed in her face.

Right, call-your-bluff time. Come on, Raig, you're as horny as a ram. No problem, even the motion would be enough, to say nothing of that pole moving up and down and Vairi's eyes fixed on you. Go for it. His hands were suddenly sweaty, his breathing fast and choppy. He saw Vairi's eyes darken and cloud with desire and knew he was going to sit on the horse and ride the pole. Briefly he thought about cum-covered jeans, before remembering the calf length, high-viz jacket hanging by the control cupboard.

"Watch and ache. Or feel free to join me." He moved close to her, deliberately invading her personal space. Her breath hitched, but she didn't move as she looked up at him steadily, that sensual quirk of her lips mesmerizing him as his body brushed hers. He hoped the hardness of her nipples and his rock-hard cock hard against her clit gave her the same experience. Sadly, he saw her fight the awareness.

"I'll watch. From here." She leaned back on the fence and folded her arms over her breasts. To hide her burgeoning nipples from any stray worker or customer who might wander past? No matter, his imagination had her stripped, leaning against the fence wearing those sparkly flats and a smile. He could tell by the skeptical look she gave him she felt he wasn't going to follow through on his words.

"Come and stand in the middle, before I set it off. Then you'll see more." And he could make sure he was on the innermost horse and farthest away from prying eyes. He held out his hand and helped her into the center. Making sure the music was switched off, he set the ride in motion, feeling Vairi's eyes following his every move as he stepped onto the platform and chose a horse.

"Conqueror," he said as, settling on the saddle, he checked the name written in flowing script around the reins. "Hope so. Ready to watch?" he called as he rode past her, and saw her nod.

Right, Raig, time to show what you can do. He edged as near to the pole as he could and felt vibrations run through him as it began to rub against his erection, the denim of his jeans increasing the friction, intensifying those erotic sensations.

God, he would never have thought he could get anywhere near coming by such a simple thing. If only they could market "Come! Ride the Ride!" They would make a fortune. Sadly, or maybe luckily, there was no way they would. It would bring every pervert for miles out of the woodwork. Meanwhile, for him now? *Enjoy the ride, Raig. Your pole on the pole.*

The sensation of being rubbed, the knowledge that Vairi's eyes were trained on him, following his tracks as much as possible, was making his climax a fast-approaching event. Even the thought that anyone could come along, see his face contorted with desire, his cock almost welded to the pole, and ask what the hell he was doing, didn't diminish his feelings. It probably intensified them. He never knew he had the incipient makings of an exhibitionist. As he flew past Vairi he spoke, his voice hoarse.

"Any time now." His cock pulsated, filled and spilled and the wet stickiness as it covered him, plus the telltale stain on his denims would be visible to anyone who looked. He shuddered and gasped until the last pulsing throb quieted. He was spent, in every which way. If he'd have been able to, he would have put his head down. As it was, he held tightly to the horse's head until his breath was less ragged and he was able to stand up without falling over.

Slowly he moved off the ride and onto the ground, almost stumbling as he hit terra firma. With deliberate movements, he switched off the ride and secured it before leaning back on the wooden cupboard.

Vairi walked across the stationary ride to where he stood and deliberately looked down to where his jeans had changed color.

"Thank you." She kissed him firmly on the lips. "That shows trust."

"That" — he returned the kiss, his tongue teasing her lips open before slipping inside — "is love. And trust. Because I do love and trust you. As you'll find out next week."

She nodded but said nothing. Just leaned into him.

"Careful, you'll get all sticky."

She moved back slightly and put a finger in the middle of the mark then moved the digit to her mouth and sucked.

His cock might have been spent, but it was interested.

"Down, boy." She grinned, looking about sixteen. "You've had your fun. How are you going to explain this away?"

"I'm not." He picked up the high-viz jacket he had removed from the cupboard and put it on. "I'll walk to the trailer and change. You coming with me?" She nodded. "We'll go out of the emergency gate there, cut behind those generators, and I'll keep my fingers crossed."

"I don't think that's going to make us very inconspicuous, do you?" She nodded at the bright yellow jacket he was shrugging into. "It might cover the evidence, but it'll cause plenty of questions. Do you have a bottle of water here?"

He took one from a small box and passed it over. Watched as she unsnapped the lid and threw the contents at him. He gasped as the coldness hit him just above the waist and ran down his torso, the denim rapidly changing to the color of the first wet patch. Vairi helped it along with a few well-chosen rubs, designed, he decided, to cause him maximum awareness and discomfort.

"That's better. It's an 'oops I tripped and flung my water all over you and I'm really sorry moment'. Visible, noticeable, explainable, and, er, subtle?"

He shivered. It might be a warm evening, but the water wasn't. "As a sledgehammer. Subtle," he elaborated as she looked blank. "But better than the jacket, I'll grant you. Right, let's go before I shrivel up and go into hibernation." He took her hand and walked swiftly toward the accommodation compound, keeping a wary lookout for anyone in the vicinity. Luckily, it seemed everyone had congregated near the Ready Room, from where, in the distance, voices could be heard. He unlocked his trailer and stood back to let her in. She hesitated, and uncharacteristically, he lost his temper.

"For fuck's sake," he snapped. "I've just jerked myself of on a bloody ride for you, and you don't trust me enough to wait inside while I get rid of the evidence? Sit there then, or go to the others. Suit yourself." He knew he'd over-reacted but for the life of him had no clue how to show Vairi that he wasn't a total prick. Instead he turned and walked inside, not looking back to see if she had followed before he carried on into the bedroom. It took a second to decide he would make enough time to shower so he stripped and went into the bathroom, turned the shower on and stood under the stream of hot, welcome water. Probably amongst the shortest showers on record, but he needed to go and add his thanks to Phil's and he'd prefer not to do it all wet and sticky.

Raid dressed as fast as he could, pulling on another pair of jeans and similar-colored T-shirt before, he went back into the lounge area. Vairi sat still on the settee and looked up as he entered.

"I'm sorry," she said quietly. "It's not you I don't trust, it's me. All I wanted to do was strip off and get into the shower with you."

He studied her pale face, seeing the regret in her eyes and the dejected droop of her shoulders. "So why didn't you?"

Vairi bit her lip and tilted her head to one side. "Because I'm a wuss and I need to be sure. I'm not doing anything until I'm sure." Determination was uppermost in her tone. "Never, ever again."

"About what?' He sat next to her and tied the laces on his trainers, glancing up as her did so.

Vairi laughed. "That's the problem. I don't have the answer yet. When I do, you'll be the first to know, after me. Until then, I'm being careful. If I do decide what I want, you'll realize it. With or without your secret coming out."

Did that mean she was beginning to think he was trustworthy? Dare he ask? Another look at her pale and resolute face decided for him. No questioning, coercing, or probing. Wait and see.

"Right then." He stood and held out his hand. "We'd better go meet the others or there will be totally erroneous speculation being bandied about. Hold on while I grab some bottles to hand out. Not an excuse, because I told Phil I would, but with luck it may waylay some gossip." He opened a cupboard and removed a dozen or so bottles of spirits. "These should do. Wait while I make a box up."

Two minutes later, the bottles safely stowed and clutching the box, he gestured for Vairi to precede him out of the trailer. As she shut the door behind them, his mobile rang.

Raig raised his eyebrows, and Vairi began to laugh as she slid her hand into the tight front pocket and, he was sure, brushed his material-covered cock on purpose as she pulled the phone out and, at his nod, answered it. He listened to her side of the conversation, obviously with Phil.

"Two minutes, we had to find a box for these bottles. I was trying to help and killed the first one. Yeah, lethal box killer, that's me. No, nothing like that. You think? I'll ask, shall I? 'Kay, I'll tell him. Sounds good to me." She ended the call and, eyes twinkling, slowly, deliberately slipped the machine back into his pocket.

"Phil says they've got Chinese takeaway, and there's a party going on. He asked were we having our own party. Did we want to just put the bottles on the step for him to collect. Cheeky sod." She laughed as she passed on the contents of the call. "I dissuaded him of that idea, but he wanted to know if he needed to run interference for us."

She didn't seem annoyed, thank goodness. Raig laughed as she checked the door was locked and slipped the key into his back pocket with a definite grope.

"Did you not think to tell him we can run our own interference with a bottle of water?"

"Damn." She clicked her fingers in mock annoyance. "I knew there was something I should have said. Ah well, another time."

"Ah, maybe not water. Something less wet. I don't mind some wetness, as er, I'm sure you guessed. Maybe a long shirt or..." He paused and winked. "Naked? High-viz jacket? You walking tight in front of me, wriggling that gorgeous butt. No, screw that. Oh shit, that didn't come out as I meant it."

Vairi doubled up, laughing at him.

"Getting yourself in a twist, Raig?" She mocked him and herself as she wriggled her butt and put her hands on his, using them to roam over the globes, and making him ultra-aware of her, her own personal scent surrounding him as she pressed close.

"Maybe I'd better not do that, or we'll need even more clean clothes, and if I went out of here in your T-shirt, that would give even more room for talk."

It'd give room for a lot more things, but he decided that it was neither the time nor the place to go into that.

Chapter Twelve

His oh-so-welcome casual workers had appreciated their food and drink, and an impromptu party had resulted in it being past two a.m. before he got to bed—alone. Unfortunately, something he was used to. *Not*, he thought as he crawled under the duvet, *something I want to stay used to.*

If this were a book, he thought savagely as he plumped his pillows up and tried to settle, *I'd pull back the covers and find Vairi waiting for me. Naked, ready and willing.* No such luck in real life. Just an alien sock he'd been looking for. How was it every time he washed socks he always ended at least one short? Then found them—sometimes in the most outlandish places? He shrugged philosophically. *Life. Get used to it, Raig.*

Finally, he found himself drifting off to sleep. To be woken by his phone telling him he had a text message. He squinted at the clock. Who the hell would be texting him at three-thirty? It was almost too much of an effort to check. Almost, but luckily, not quite.

Now there was no way he would sleep.

Got home. Couldn't sleep. Decided to have a glass of red wine. Thought of you and your pole. Spilled the wine.

Before he had time to answer, the next text arrived.

Got the white wine to put on the red. Had a swig. Wished it was you I was drinking!

Fuck! *Now she tells me*, he thought

Scrubbed the carpet. Nice and clean now.

Oh good. Why was she telling him that? He found out.

Clean enough to 'eat' off.

Right! Now she added that. His mind was whirling.

How do you feel about carpet burns?

How the hell did he answer that without incriminating himself?

Try anything once, I say. When and where?

There was silence from his phone. He waited impatiently.

I'll let you know.

Finally, he slept. The sun shining through the gap along the bottom of the window blind woke him up as it moved across his face. He stirred and felt...his hands grasping his cock, the stickiness there telling him that what he had decided was an amazing dream had been an amazing wet dream... Oh *shit!* As fast as he could he unglued his hands and grabbed a damp cloth that had mysteriously appeared on the bedside table. A thought struck him. He picked up his phone and scrolled through the messages. Text sex and a half. Would he ever be able to look her in the face? He shot a quick glance at his phone and realized his texts had been answered, and some! He fell back onto the pillows and laughed until his ribs ached, before starting to reread.

I'll look forward to it coming.

He couldn't remember sending that.

Oh, so will I. You going to come for me? Or shall I come for you?

Where am I coming?

He would be coming soon if he wasn't careful—his cock was needy, rubbing the duvet as his hands moved on the phone. He scrolled to see her reply.

Up to you. What are you up for?

He looked at his impatient cock. At this rate, about three minutes.
He scrolled to see his answer of the night before.

You.

Nice to know. How long are you up for?

About six inches.

How long are you around?

Three and a half.

Hours?

He chuckled to himself as he reread that answer from Vairi. Remembered his answer before he read it again.

Inches.

Ah.

There had been several minutes before the next text. He was about to give up and take himself in hand, an unusual occurrence for him—he'd rather go without.

Are you being a jerk now?

Sure am. Do you need a hand?

Don't think you have one to spare.

Sure I have. I can work single-handed.

Are you?

He had been, and he was again. One hand held his phone, and he used the other to slowly rub up and down his cock, mimicking his actions of earlier.

Oh, I am. How are you doing?

Slowly, deeply. It's very wet here. How is it with you?

The same as before. He was hot, hard and horny. Ready to come. He looked at the following text.

Very wet. It's coming fast.

As it was now. His hand moved faster, harder, tighter. He groaned as his cock swelled, throbbed and spilled over his hand, his groin, his thighs. He waited until his breathing had regulated before he read on.

Same here. Very wet, very hot. The change in temperature has come. Amazing how swiftly the change occurred.

Happened here as well. It's very hot, wet, and sticky.

So good to know we both experienced the same thing.

He agreed with that.

So, time to stop being a jerk and a handyman and dry off?

Yup. And you?

A handy-woman, of course. Done the washing up, so all clean and tidy here. Good night? xx.

The best. And morning. He read the last text as his hand curled loosely around his resting cock.

Oh yes. I'm going to follow your example and wash and tidy up. A good handyman never forgets his tools. Good night, sleep tight xx.

Time to take care of his tools again. He got up and headed into the shower and spent just long enough under the spray as necessary before he switched off the water and toweled himself dry. At this rate his water bill would double, he seemed to spend so much time under the spray. Now he was running late, and although he had told Phil there was no hurry to get together, he had other things to do before they met.

The first was another text.

Sleep well?

He didn't have to wait long for his answer.

And you? Not too stiff?

Not anymore. All in hand and taken care of.

LOL. So glad. Gotta go. It's wet here again, and I need to get things dry. C U sometime soon?

Thursday. 7pm. I'll pick you up. It's important.

Oh, OK.

There were no more texts. It was time to get to work on emails from Kenny. Raig had a lot to do before their meeting on Monday. Also, with only two more days before his time with the fair was over for another year, there was a great amount to discuss with Phil. First and foremost was Phil's salary increase, and he was worth every penny of it. Then there were loose ends to tie up and arrangements to be made to confirm the new rides being bought for the following season. All things he had input in.

Phil was faintly green and nursing a large cup of black coffee. He glared at Raig as he entered the Ready Room and closed the door quietly behind him, grinning at the morose man behind the desk.

"Sore head? Something to do with spinning the bottle?" He referred to the drinking game that had been played the previous evening. Phil had seemed to be on the receiving end rather a lot.

Phil grunted. "How the hell did it never stop at you?"

"I cheated," Raig said complacently. "I knew where I stood, gravity worked for me and not the bottle."

"Bastard." Phil took two painkillers from a blister pack and swallowed them with a gulp of coffee. "My mouth is a parrot's cage. Yuck."

"Poor Phil. And we need to talk business as well." Raig poured himself coffee and sat on a chair by the desk. He glanced down at his newly washed jeans and managed not to blush or swell inside them. Stonewashed denim would never be the same again. "Are you up for it?" Oops, wrong choice of words. Luckily Phil had no idea and just nodded.

"Yeah. Self-inflicted misery is no excuse for not working. By the way, we can open the food stalls tonight. And Tessa has been given a written and final warning. Thought I'd be a little bit lenient. Think she got a real scare."

Raig nodded and felt his phone vibrate. He excused himself and took it out of his pocket. To his disappointment, it wasn't from Vairi. However, it gave him almost as much pleasure. An email from Stevie, her producer, who had been one of the helpers the previous night. It was short and to the point.

Saturday. Studio 3. Eleven fifty, for twelve thirty. Saturday Spotlight On. You game? Let me know. P.S. tell Phil he is awesome at Twister.

He raised his eyebrow as he looked at Phil. "Twister?"

"Oh, sheesh." Phil groaned, albeit with a faint smile on his lips. "Before you appeared, I beat Stevie hollow. Probably why he got his own back with spin the bottle. Er, where were you, or don't I ask?"

"You can ask. Whether you believe what I tell you is up to you. Vairi spilled water over me and I had to change."

"New name for it." Phil's lips twitched. "Doubt the others knew how long you'd been. I, however, know how long it takes to lock the carousel up."

"Good. And you will keep it to yourself."

Phil laughed and groaned. "No fair, no laughing. Okay, let's work, anything to stop me feeling sorry for myself. Or remembering the legs on that redhead." His eyes darkened for a moment. "Oh, my head."

Redhead? He didn't remember any redhead. But then, he'd only had eyes for Vairi. The whole casts of *The Vagina Monologues* and *Calendar Girls* could have walked past naked and it wouldn't have registered on his radar. They set to work.

By the time they had argued, compromised and agreed it was mid-afternoon, and Raig was hungry. When Raig suggested they ring for an Indian meal, Phil agreed with a heartfelt "oh yeah". It wasn't long before they were sniffing the air like the Bisto Kids as several containers were delivered. Raig remembered the text from Stevie. The opportunity sounded interesting. He fished his phone out as Phil served up the curries. Sent a brief text — *Elucidate* — and began to eat while he waited for an answer. It wasn't long in coming. But not by text. He had just cleared his plate when his phone rang.

"I need to take this, Phil, sorry."

"No problem." Phil gathered up the empty cartons. "*I*

need to do the walkabout anyway. I'll leave you to it." He swept the cartons into the rubbish bin and, with a wave, left the trailer, closing the door very carefully.

"O'Shea." In case it wasn't Stevie. It was.

"Oh shit, must I really introduce myself as Runciman? It's Stevie here. Er, Runciman."

Raig laughed. "Yeah, sorry, Stevie, I forgot to add you to my address list. What's this Saturday Spotlight On thing?"

"A new concept for the show. Not new exactly, but we haven't run it for about a year. A fifteen-minute spot where Vairi chats to someone live about their life, and people can email their questions in for the guest to answer—or not. I thought the fair would be a good thing to talk about. How you spend time working with it, and what you do when you are not there."

Oh hell. What could he say?

"Did you mention this to Vairi?" he asked cautiously. Was this her way of trying to find what he did when he wasn't riding the carousel? He couldn't believe that, she was too open to find out in such a way. His faith in her was confirmed by Stevie's next comment.

"Nope. It was just an idea I had after last night. I know it's short notice and you might not fancy doing it, but…"

Raig ran his hand through his hair and twisted his earring, something he often did when he was trying to decide a course of action. This was tricky. He liked Stevie, he'd helped him out of the mess the night before and he'd like to repay the favor. But, and it was a big but, was this the way? Could he do it justice when so much of his life had to be undisclosed? He made up his mind.

"You need to check Vairi is okay with it, Stevie. We're still not really back to normal—whatever normal is. If she wants to go ahead, then I'll do it." After all he'd been adept about being economical with the truth for a good few years now, surely he could manage for a bit longer? It was the fact it was Vairi he would be lying to that made him hesitate. "I'll wait for you to get back to me." They exchanged a few platitudes before Stevie rang off with the promise to let him know whether the interview would go ahead or not. In a strange way, he was optimistic it would. He would have to watch what he said, but then, hadn't he been doing that since puberty? It would give him time with Vairi as well, which could only be good. Frustrating, but good. Meanwhile, back to the grind. He spent the next two hours doing manual labor, and almost enjoyed the feeling of working muscles not otherwise used. Unfortunately, combined with the muscles he had used the previous night, by the time he finished, he ached all over.

A very large coffee and a set of stretching exercises went a long way toward helping him feel reasonably agile before he changed for another evening of all the fun of the fair. It was unfortunate all the fun would not include Vairi. As he made a sandwich for a quick snack, his mobile rang. He had entered Stevie's number, and it came up as the caller. His palms were damp as he took the call. He hadn't realized how much Vairi accepting him on the show would mean to him. He rubbed his hands on his jeans.

"Hi."

"Hi back." Now the roof of his mouth was dry and his tongue seemed stuck there. He had to swallow before he could speak.

"You're on."

It took a few seconds for the simple statement to register. "Vairi okay with that?"

He could almost see Stevie's grin. "Yup, said it would be a pleasure to tie you up in knots."

That sounded like Vairi. He liked the sound of that statement, although, he thought with regret, she probably didn't mean it quite the way it sounded. Since when had he been into true bondage anyway? Since never. Now he had a feeling he could be persuaded. There was no way he was going to pass that information to her, especially not via Stevie. Instead he settled for a banal, "Fine, I'll be there," ignoring Stevie's choked-back laugh.

"Good show. I'll email you probable questions so you can have a think about them. Let me know if they're the sort of things you are happy talk about. Then, if all's fine, we'll see you tomorrow."

"Yeah." He finished the call and tapped the phone thoughtfully on one jean-covered thigh. Was he doing the right thing? *Oh well,* he shrugged inwardly. He'd know that the following night. Before then he had a ride to oversee and an All the Fun of the Fair Family Fun Day to get through on the morrow. Not until after that would he have time to think about how he was going to manage to be so near Vairi again and not jump her.

The Family Fun Day proved to be so busy he didn't have time to eat, let alone think. Having mentioned to Phil he wouldn't be around at close-down, he wondered why Phil came to relieve him from the stall he was covering a good hour before his break.

"Phone call from Stevie. You haven't given him the all clear on the probable questions he emailed to you. He needs an answer."

"F — Er, darn." He pulled himself up in time, remembering the age of most of the bodies trying to win a coconut. "I forgot all about it. What's the time?"

"Half past four. I told him you'd get back to him as soon as. Now go, eat, drink and email. Don't come back for at least an hour. The kids' session will finish soon, and we should get a bit of a lull then."

Raig nodded his thanks and swung his long legs over the counter of the stall. If he managed to get to his trailer without being stopped, it would be a miracle. Anyone who had wanted free tickets after the help-night had been given them, and already several people had stopped when they saw him to say thanks. He was berating himself regarding the potential questions Stevie had sent when he caught a glimpse of long dark curls, and his heart jumped.

Stupid, it's not Vairi. She'd be at home, not at the fair. He was right. The owner of the ringlets turned. He was taken aback by the stab of disappointment he felt when he saw a total stranger. *Man, you've got it bad.*

He had it even worse when he looked over the questions. Double entendre, innuendo and plain, pure sex! There was no way these would be asked on the radio. Then he saw the next line.

I wrote these. Stevie didn't see them, now his questions are...

Sneaky. He skimmed the reasonably innocuous questions Stevie proposed and wrote two individual emails, the first to Stevie agreeing the questions. The second to Vairi, he simply wrote—

To be answered in full on Thursday next week. Meanwhile: 1, yes; 2, no; 3, I will if you will; and 4, 13.

He pressed send before finding some food.

Half an hour later, he felt a lot better when he saw an email from Vairi.

Have we moved to e-mail sex now? Oh goody. I'm well up for it if you are.

It made him laugh before he replied honestly.

It's so hard, but yup, I'm up for it.

Was he ever! Up, hard and straining his jeans.

How about you?

Well, it's not really dry around here. Looking forward to exchanging views on this later.

Oh, so was he. Before he had that chance he had to work. At least for a few hours. Willing his cock to behave and calm down, not easy when his body was clamoring for release, he went back to the fairground. To be swamped by people, problems and perversity.

Arrgh. Give me strength, he thought as for the fourth time he told Tessa Willows — she of the mushroom soup fiasco — that whatever Phil said went. "Nothing to do with me," he said firmly as she protested at her written warning. He eventually ran out of patience.

"Tessa, if I was the boss here, you'd have been out without the warning," he said forcefully.

She sniffed scornfully, muttering something about problems ahead. Yeah, yeah, no doubt about that. Watching her stalk off to her caravan, its walls covered with endorsements about her prowess and pronouncements, he sighed. Truthfully, he could do with a positive endorsement of his actions. That notwithstanding, he had work to do before he ducked out and headed for the radio station.

Work proved to be problematic. Not just for him. First of all, he had to try to be polite to a couple who were startled when the music got faster and dropped their chips. They argued that therefore they should get a free pass on the rides. The offer, without prejudice, of a replacement bag of chips, had not been received well. Tough, he was sick of people wanting something for nothing and certainly didn't envy Phil, having this shit day after day. Meanwhile he had an interview to do. With a wave to Phil, as one of the fairground workers relieved him, he headed back to his trailer to get ready for what might be the most important hour of his life to date, before heading into town.

He dressed carefully — carefully but casually. Why it mattered he wasn't sure, but it did. Whatever happened during the rest of the evening, he would look the part. Even if in all honestly he had no idea what the part was.

Chapter Thirteen

He was early. Of course he was. Sweating, shit-scared early. If anyone commented on it with any variation of 'oh, you've come early', he might just do that! Or else throw something.

A nervous young girl approached him. The way her eyes darted over him, encased in his favorite old, faded denims which faithfully followed the line of his body, his black, fitted, V-neck T-shirt and canvas shoes, he knew she was weighing him up. By the roll of her eyes, it seemed he had been found wanting. He hadn't thought any more about what to wear after his initial 'casual and comfortable' decision. When he was enjoying his weeks with the fair, his uniform was jeans and T-shirt, just as a business suit was appropriate wear on other occasions.

"Er, um, Mr. O'Shea?"

He wasn't sure how many other people they were expecting at almost midnight, but nodded politely instead of following his inclination to say, "No, I'm a Womble." After all, might not a Womble be interviewed after him? "That's me. And you are?"

"Oh, er, I'm Cathy, the dogsbody." She grinned, then seemed to hear what she had said and blushed, her face the color of the skirt she was wearing. "Um, I mean..."

He helped her. "You do everything they need to get the show out."

"Oh no." She sounded horrified. "That's up to Vairi and Stevie, er, I mean, Ms..."

He did laugh then. "Vairi and Stevie is fine. They are friends. I'm Raig." He held out his hand and had it gently shaken. He waited.

"Oh, right, I need to take you to Stevie. They're doing the last-minute checks before the show."

He followed her along several corridors before she knocked on a door and ushered him in. Through the glass that made up one wall, he could see Vairi. She glanced up, smiled wickedly, and went back to what she was doing.

Stevie laughed at the look that passed from her to Raig.

"Not so sure this will work now," he said, still laughing. "Just as well we have a delay on transmission."

"Why live anyway?" It was something Raig had wondered about.

"So you can answer emails that come in."

Ah, he'd forgotten that bit. How many people had she primed to write in? He didn't realize he had spoken aloud until Stevie answered him.

"Doesn't matter. You can choose not to answer. Hell, if we get a lot you won't have time to answer them all anyway. Just remember, anything you say will be noted and may be held against you."

Yeah, right, now that he could believe.

"Gee, thanks. All I need. The correctness squad looking over my shoulder."

"You'll be fine." Stevie clapped him on the shoulder. "Right, let's go through what you need to do."

Five minutes later, Raig wished he'd stayed at home. He was supposed to be taking a break from all this stuff. He said as much to Stevie, who merely laughed and looked confused.

"Eh?"

Damn, damn and bloody double damn. Of course Stevie had no idea of his other occupations. "I work as an investment banker," he said hastily. "When I'm not at the fair. Lots of questions to answer."

"Ah. Well I don't think the punters'll be asking about hedge funds or stocks and shares. Right. Ready?"

Raig scowled and knew he looked and felt like a sulky

schoolboy. *Grow up, Raig. Suck it up, you could have said no and you didn't. Your decision, your choice, your problem.*

"Right." There was nothing else he could say. He followed Stevie into the next room, put on the earphones as instructed, and waited.

"Now, peeps, as I mentioned earlier, tonight we're having one of our Saturday Spotlight On interviews. Although it's been pointed out to me that we should call it Sunday Spotlight. Ah well, I'll take that up with Stevie. So let me introduce you to Raig O'Shea, entrepreneur extraordinaire and fair owner. Welcome, Raig. Glad you were able to come." Her smile was still wicked. He aimed for the same expression as he spoke mildly.

"My pleasure, you're worth coming for."

Vairi coughed. Next door Stevie choked with laughter and shook his finger at them both.

"Oh... So if you have any questions, you know where to send them. First a question from me." Her smile sent sensual messages to his groin, making his cock harden and his mind wander to what she was — or was not — wearing beneath the sexy sundress she had on, the bright orange and purples searing his retina, imprinting her on his mind.

"How do you have the stamina to do all you do?"

The devilment in her eyes was such a challenge. His response was, he hoped, equally so. "I work hard at everything I do. I enjoy hard work, thrive on it, in fact. Everything I come up with, everything I achieve, is what I intend. Practice makes perfect is the credo I use. What about you?"

"I think that's a perfect expression. Now, let's have some music and wait for those emails to come rolling in." As the music began, they heard Stevie's call to them.

"Stop that, you two. Now. No more overt innuendo please. Let's tone it down, eh?"

Raig laughed and acknowledged the plea with a shrug. "Please, sir, she started it." Vairi responded by sticking out her tongue. He growled. "Oh, yes please."

"Enough. Here's the first emails coming in. They're okay, I think, but up to you."

A sheaf of papers was handed to him. He scanned the first couple, gave Stevie a thumbs-up, and passed them to Vairi. All very innocuous. The fourth one made him raise his eyebrows. He grabbed a pencil and scored through it, writing briefly, *Tell them to f-off. Nothing comes for free...oops!* Vairi read the email and the comment.

"Stevie, why the hell did you decide to pass this one through? Utter crap."

Stevie shrugged. "All get passed through, up to Raig if he wants to tell some tosser that he worked his socks off to get where he is, and no, he isn't going to give a handout to him." The email had been nothing more than a gimme-something-for-nothing plea.

"Music stopping, opening the mike," Vairi warned. "Well, that was *Money, Money, Money* from the musical *Mamma Mia*. Now, folks, my guest tonight is Raig O'Shea, and your emails have been rolling in. So first off is from Pat Sinclair, who wants to know which part of your life you prefer."

Half an hour later, Raig pulled off his headphones in relief. There had been no more innuendo, no tricky questions, just total admiration for Vairi's professionalism, as she had seamlessly slipped between music and chat. He'd had to think fast on more than one occasion to answer a question put in such a way as to stretch him.

He exited the studio and was beckoned into the equivalent of the fair's Ready Room, where Stevie sat monitoring all that was happening.

"Lord of all you survey," Raig commented, taking both the seat and the mineral water offered.

"Huh, with Vairi? You must be joking. I'm just here for the ride. Oh fuck, no, I'm not."

Raig roared with laughter and commented, "No, that's my role, I think."

"Hell, Raig, you're good for her. I haven't seen Vairi so animated in ages. Whatever you're doing, don't stop. Shit and crap. That's both feet in it now. I'm saying no more. Except she'll be finished in an hour. Are you going to hang around? I usually run her home, but if you want to try your chance?" He had raised an eyebrow in an interrogative gesture.

Raig nodded. "My pleasure."

It was strange, sitting and watching her as she bantered her way through an hour of chat and music, knowing thousands of other people had her voice with them wherever they were. By the time the program was over, his admiration for her had grown tenfold. He said as much to her as she joined him and Stevie once the program finished.

She curtseyed mockingly. "Thank you, kind sir. I do my humble best."

He leaned into her and spoke into her ear. "Oh, Vairi My Queen, your best is so not humble." He sneaked a kiss and laughed as she nipped his mouth. "Are you ready for your lift home? I'm your chauffeur this evening. Stevie has a hot date with his wife and a mug of cocoa. In that order."

If looks could kill, Raig felt he would be asking what Stevie's favorite flowers were. Vairi's glare was truly frightening. It didn't faze Stevie, who just laughed. "She'll be glad to see me home in time to make the cocoa for her."

"Hmm. I must say I've *never* heard it called that before." Her tone of voice was grumpy, but the glint in her eyes belied it. "Fair enough. I'd be pleased to accept you as my chauffeur, Raig. To let Stevie go home and have his, er, cocoa. See you on Wednesday, Stevie. Remind your beloved we have a coffee date tomorrow, and she's picking me up. *No* innuendo needed. I've heard it all now. Huh, cocoa." She shook her head, and with a wave, allowed Raig to usher her out of the room and toward the car park entrance.

"What made you ask me to be here tonight?" he queried as he activated the central locking of the car and held her door open. She settled into the seat.

"What made you agree to come?" she parried as he joined her in the car.

"It seems I'll come for you anywhere, my love." He started the engine, enjoying the look of pleasure and confusion on her face.

"You, Rake O'Shea, are just that. Rake by name, rake by nature."

"Not anymore. Only for you, Vairi. I'll be your rake, no one else's. As and how you want." They sat in not altogether comfortable silence until the car drew up outside her house. "Am I coming in?'

"Coming in where? Me? Nope. My house? Nope."

"Ah well." He hadn't really expected a yes. "I'll not be coming anywhere or anyhow then. I'll see you safely to your doorstep." He walked around the car and opened the passenger door for her before escorting her to her front door and waiting until she was inside.

"Night, my love. I'll see you on Thursday." He leaned in again, chest brushing breasts, and kissed her until her mouth opened and allowed him to slip his tongue inside. A moan escaped from her as he deepened the kiss, feeling her nipples peak and his body respond in return. This was not good for the state of his mind, let alone for the state of his cock. He didn't need Tessa Willows to foresee a cold shower appearing in his near future. Reluctantly, he ended the kiss, pleased to see Vairi's eyes clouded with desire. It was satisfying to know he affected her as much as she affected him. "I'll wait until I hear the door lock, and I won't drive away until your bedroom light goes on."

"Peeping Tom? No chance. I shut my curtains." She closed the door in his face.

He was chuckling as he reached the car, noting Vairi hadn't mentioned he'd changed his mode of travel. He'd decided the bike stood less of a chance to take her home, so he'd chosen to use his car instead. With hindsight, he was pleased he'd done so. The feeling of Vairi pressed hard against him and knowing there would be nothing else offered would have been excruciating. As it was, her scent permeated his senses and the memory of her long, elegant legs caressed by her flirty skirt, teasing him, was enough to make him uncomfortably aroused. He drove off, conscious of his rock-hard cock pushing at its confining denim—and even more conscious of the lack of opportunity to help it out.

His phone was vibrating as he drew up in the parking compound. He stopped the engine, removed the key, got out and locked the car before checking the text.

Not such a jerk!

Thanks. No answer to that. Before he had formatted a return text, his phone signaled another one.

So glad you were able to come.

He could certainly answer that.

I'll come for you anytime. Definitely not a jerk anymore.

Finally, as he reached his trailer, the next text appeared.

Good. Glad to hear it. So nice when you come for me. Hope you have a good night's sleep.

She certainly knew how to try to have the last word. This time, he would let her. After locking the door, he undressed and got into bed, to sleep and dream before waking up refreshed.

* * * *

Sunday, his last day with the fair, passed quietly. It was always a wrench to leave. The fair was ingrained in him, the memories of the child strengthened with the more recent memories of the adult. But he was honest enough to admit that there was not a sufficient challenge to keep him. He needed the cut and thrust of the rest of his life. How he would cope when that half ceased to exist remained to be seen. Raig was confident his world would be fuller, brighter, especially if Vairi was prepared to become part of it. Without her, its brilliance would be diminished. However, he reasoned, the change was well overdue. It was something he had been fighting.

He left the site early on Monday morning. With most of the fair having departed for the next venue, only Jonny and Phil were around to see him go, the way he liked it. By lunchtime he was home, had parked his trailer in his extensive drive, and driven the car then the bike into the garage. With a special hitch on his trailer he'd been able to move everything in one go. Exhausting, a slow drive, but oh, so worth it.

Now, he was revved up and ready to go headfirst into his meetings. By two p.m., immaculate in a dark gray suit, crisp white shirt and striped tie, he was in his office, dictating rapidly with one eye on the clock. As far as he was concerned, the time spent inside that stuffy room was a necessary evil—the time he was going to spend in another office later on was purely necessary.

"Right," he said finally. "That's it. I'll be back in the morning." He smiled at his P.A., a balding, middle-aged Scot called, of all things, Alberto MacInnes. "And, Berto? Thanks for holding the fort."

He remembered Alberto's, '*Och, you're welcome, it wasnae problem*', as he drove across town to his next meeting, the important one of the day. Nothing seemed to faze Berto, not even his boss disappearing for weeks at a time with only an odd email for contact. He made a mental note to up his salary. Without Berto he wouldn't be as easy in his mind about the problems that were sure to follow.

Raig parked his car, took up a briefcase and, after locking up, walked briskly toward an anonymous brick office block, looking like any one of a million white-collar workers on their way to yet another meeting. He entered the foyer, then made his way up the stairs to an office marked simply

O'Shea Enterprises.

Kenny was waiting for him, a pot of coffee steaming away at the side of the room. He poured a mug and handed it over. Raig nodded his thanks.

"Cheers. Right, where are we at?"

Kenny half smiled. "In a hurry, are we?"

He nodded. "Are we ever, Kenny. This goes out on Thursday, no excuses. Where do I start?"

"Understood, Raig. Okay, so, we'll start like this…"

Raig listened intently, occasionally questioning or disagreeing with something he was told. At one point he thumped the table.

"No. No, no, no. Definitely not. No way. It finishes today. Tomorrow at the latest. Michael Dooley is finished. Not let off to resurrect himself later. He is done. Nothing less is an acceptable outcome. My future life is contingent on that."

Kenny sighed and relented. "Fine, fine. Let's get started then. Are you ready for a late night?"

In reply, Raig pulled off his tie, dropping it on top of his already discarded jacket, and loosened the top two buttons of his shirt. "Let's get on with it," he answered tersely. "Secure it so tightly no one can undo it."

If there was ever anyone any good at tying things in knots, it was Kenny. Raig felt like an amateur compared to him. A happy amateur, as a couple of hours later he ran through what still had to be done.

"That works," he finally said as Kenny indicated they had done all they could for the day. "You're ace. Tomorrow?"

"Eight a.m.," Kenny confirmed. "Be ready for the shit to hit the fan and the ruckus to start. Watch your back."

Raig had no worries on that score—that was a certainty. "No problem. See you at eight." He left the building and checked his car via his remote security option, feeling stupid as he did but knowing it made sense. As he drove home, the reality suddenly hit him. If he didn't get this sorted, he virtually could say 'bye-bye, Vairi'. That was *not* an option.

Without warning, the need to hear her voice hit him hard

and violently. To such a degree the car swerved as his heart jolted. Then he wondered if his lack of concentration was the only reason he had swerved.

Had he been found out? Was the swerve not due to his bad driving, but a bullet in a tire? Defective brake pads? Something even more sinister?

Get a grip, Raig, he told himself, willing his heart rate to slow and his adrenaline to decrease. *If no one has sussed out the connection between you and Michael Dooley by now, how likely is it to happen just days before that connection is severed forever? You're not playing the leading role in a thriller, tension on overload, designed to grab the reader by the throat and keep them interested. This is your life.* He remembered a TV show of his youth. *Without Eamonn Andrews, Michael Aspel or whoever standing nearby with a big red book.*

It was oh-so-easy to say, less easy to accept. By the time he got home and used the remote to open then secure the gates after him, he had a neck ache from all the swiveling from side to side he'd done. To say nothing of an even greater need to hear Vairi's voice.

Chapter Fourteen

Raig walked into the house, already trying to connect to her mobile number. Sod the 'I'm going to be noble and not contact her' bit. He needed to hear her voice like a man in the desert needed water. What were the odds she wouldn't answer?

Luckily he didn't need them. He'd hardy pressed Call before his phone was answered. "Raig? Are you okay?" She sounded breathless, worried.

"Missing you. Why? What's wrong?"

He heard her sigh. "You tell me. Honestly, Raig, I'm the last person to believe in feelings and all that stuff, but a few minutes ago I felt, well, weird, and thought I had to ring you. I was just trying to connect when you rang me. Spooky or what?" She forced a laugh. He didn't think she managed it very well.

"Not spooky," he assured her. "It shows how connected we are." Dare he tell her it seemed they had experienced the need simultaneously? Maybe not. He had an idea that would be one step too far for her.

"Where are you, Raig?" She sounded hesitant, as if she had no right to ask. He felt a rush of anger directed at himself. *For fuck's sake, Raig, this is the woman you profess to love, and she's worried to even ask that? Not good.*

"I'm at home," he replied. "Just got in after meetings, meetings and more meetings." There was silence. He ran through what he had said in his mind. Shit. That could be in Timbuktu as far as she knew. Economical with the truth? He was a joke. Tighter than a miser's wallet. Quickly he named the town. "Took a couple of hours to get back, because I had the bike and stuff to tow. I live on a hill, I can see the sea. You'll see when you visit."

"Am I visiting then?" Not much emotion projected to him. His own fault.

"I hope you'll do more than just visit, my love. I know I've a lot to explain, to ask you to understand." His composure cracked. "Hell, Vairi, if you don't understand, I don't know what I'll do. Thursday is so important, you wouldn't believe. When I pick you up, will you come here with me? Let me explain it all here? Please?"

Her breathing was loud in the room.

"Why Thursday? Why not now?"

Was that pleading he heard?

"Ah, love. I so wish I could. But please, I am asking for your faith and trust." He paused, feeling his way with care. "Do I ever know how much I'm asking of you, but *a chuisle*" —he used the endearment on purpose— "I love you. I'm trying to make sure we can have a safe life, full of trust and love. It's to be hoped that on Thursday, I'll be able to offer you it."

"Safe? As in boring? Or as in not dangerous?"

Right, Raig, your chance to show this famous trust you think you are giving to her. "The latter, love. To keep us safe and not be at risk of harm, I'm asking for you to keep faith in me."

"Until Thursday?" she asked finally. "Really?"

"Really, mind you, I'm hoping you'll have faith in me a long while after that as well." There was humor in his voice, humor he intended her to hear. He decided to push his luck. "I'm hoping I'll have a lot more than faith *in* you, my love. You know, my—"

"I get the picture." There was laughter in her voice, and it gave him hope. "Think higher thoughts, Rake."

"Oh, I do. Then I get to your breasts, that kissable mouth. Oh, my higher thoughts are just as erotic as my lower ones."

This time there was a definite sigh down the phone. "So are mine. Oh, Raig." She stopped. He willed her to carry on. "I'll come," she said finally. "With you. To your house."

"As well as come with me. In my…" He paused, listened to her laugh. "House. Or anywhere else you fancy. I'm open to suggestions, love. So can I pick you up early? Go for lunch?"

"I guess you can." To him, hopeful and impatient, he thought he heard love in the tone. Decided not to comment on how she spoke, but on what she spoke.

"Good, I'll pick you up at noon. It will be a pleasure to show you my neck of the woods, show you —" He stopped suddenly, accepting he was getting ahead of himself. He'd been about to say, 'Show you where we will live'. Hell, he didn't even know if they would be in the same vicinity as each other at the end of the week, much less planning a life together. "My house."

"Sounds good. Look, I'd better let you go." Vairi sounded as reluctant as him to end the call. "Are you sure nothing is up?"

"Now I've spoken to you, something is very up. Sadly, it will have to be disappointed. Deflated even." Her gurgle of laughter sent his body into overdrive. How on earth was he going to last until Thursday? He was not even going to entertain the thought that nothing might happen then or afterward. "Vairi My Queen, I can't begin to tell you how much I love you. How much I want us to be together, a couple. I just hope" — he paused — "pray you will understand everything about why I've been less than open. Believe me, it's been the hardest thing not to tell you everything, but until Thursday, I can't. Even then, I guess there will be some things you won't understand. I just have to hope our love will be strong enough to carry us through."

The silence was so long he began to wonder if she had hung up. Finally, softly, she spoke. "So do I."

How the hell was he going to sleep after that admission? Surprisingly well. He woke just after six a.m., refreshed and ready to face whatever was thrown at him. Just as well. Kenny was morose when they met up.

"Lost a pound and found a penny?" he asked him, using one of his gran's favorite sayings for a long face.

Kenny grimaced. "Almost. The powers that be want Mickey D to carry on."

"No way! No. *Fucking*. Way. *Nada. Non. Niet. Nein*. No! *Comprenez?*"

"I do. They don't."

"So?" He was incensed. "How are they going to succeed in that? My contract is up. Do they not remember that? Ended yesterday, fortuitously. And, Kenny, they needn't think someone else can take over the role. Tell them to check the contract. Michael Dooley is dead. Well dead. Fuck, give me the phone. I'll tell them." He held out his hand.

Kenny shook his head. "I'm ahead of you. We have had the conversation, believe me. They are not happy. Mickey D hasn't only done a good job, he's increased ratings." His tone was dry.

"Mickey D hasn't only done a good job, he's done such a good job he's had death threats. Do they not accept that?" Raig's tone was incredulous. "Fuck, Kenny, what planet are they on? Mickey D needs killing off. Disappearing forever. Sod the ratings. Life is more important than fucking ratings."

Kenny held his hands up. "Hey, man, don't shoot the messenger. I'm one of the good guys. I've put my neck on the line here. Told them it's no-go. Michael Dooley is dead and buried. Up to them to believe it. Having said that, Thursday, nine p.m. is a go. Late change to listed program, et cetera."

Raig inhaled. Exhaled slowly, calming himself with difficulty. It was oh-so hard to understand the morons who didn't value a person's safety. He did, and he would fight for it. Every time.

"Okay. So, what now?"

Kenny's voice was gleeful. "Let's go for it. Let's put the nail in the coffin. The demise of Michael Dooley. R.I.P. End of."

"With you there. Let's do it."

They did. They worked, argued and plotted.

Finally, both were satisfied. *It has been,* Raig thought, *the most stressful eight hours of my life, and that's saying something.* Michael Dooley would not live to fight another day.

Raig stretched. If he wasn't so tired, so utterly wasted, he would have essayed a high five. As it was, he simply grinned. "Oh *yes.* At last. I think we've done it, Kenny. Killed him off. Time to move on. If I've lost this source of income, I'd better give a bit more attention to my other source. Poor Berto, I sometimes wonder if he thinks I'm real. So, onward, upward and forward. For something better."

"As in Vairi, I guess?"

He nodded. "Fuck, I hope so."

Kenny smiled. "For your sake, so do I. Keep me in the loop. Now fuck off and go to bed. Sleep the sleep of the justified."

If only. It was all well and good to say something like that, not as easy to do so. He knew he was in the right, knew he had done the right thing and knew the rest of his life was now beginning. It was out of his hands as to whether it would be a happy, successful, safe life.

He drove home that night in a strange mood. God, how he missed Vairi and hoped to hell he had done everything he could to facilitate their life together. He needed to hear her voice. Once again he found himself calling her as he entered his house. Once again she answered immediately, sounding as if she had been waiting for his call.

"Hi."

"Hi, yourself. What are you up to?"

Her laugh was deep, breathy and fucking sexy, sending messages to his cock he had no chance of picking up. "Personally? Up to nothing. Feeling a bit fed up, to be honest." She seemed to hesitate. "I've got a lot to think about, and it isn't easy. What I'm thinking."

Someone else struggling with the meaning of life. There was no answer he could give, no help to proffer. "Have you thought anything profitable?"

"I think so. Maybe. We'll see." Her voice became happier, more upbeat, as if whatever decision she had made she could now forget about and move on. "So, my Rake, what have you been up to tonight?"

He took heart from her method of address. "Working, my love. And it *was* profitable. I'll have a lot to show you on Thursday."

"There's an offer!" Her laugh through the phone was like music. "I shall look forward to it. Will you be listening to me tomorrow? Sending me emails? Stevie says he'll miss not having them if you don't."

Was that a plea in her voice, or was it his imagination? "Of course I'll be listening. Tell Stevie I'll send an email in just for him. What's your theme?"

"Ah now, that would be telling. You'll need to wait until tomorrow night to find out."

"It will be hard."

He hadn't meant the innuendo until he heard that sexy gurgle of laughter again. "Oh, I do hope so."

He laughed back. "Seems to be a permanent state of affairs at the moment. It's very hard." He paused. "Without you to help."

Vairi sighed. "We'll see if I can do anything to soften the situation. Soon. Now, I'm off to bed. With Plato."

"His book?" It seemed heavy reading for bedtime, but who was he to judge?

"Nope, my teddy bear. 'Night. Sleep tight."

"I wish I were Plato."

Her laughter kept him upbeat as he showered and got into bed. He would listen to her show, send in some emails and get ready to welcome her home.

* * * *

The thought of hearing her voice for two hours late at night haunted his thoughts all day. In a good way. He had surprised Alberto with both his thanks for holding the fort so often and his immediate pay rise. His own surprise was the amount of work they were able to get through. Both of them were inspired. By four o'clock he felt justified in calling it a day.

"That's enough for today, Berto. You must be sick of the sight of me. Shall I start looking for something to keep me out of the office?"

His P.A. laughed and shook his head. "No, don't do that. I'm happy to have you here. Don't get me wrong, I'm happy to keep things ticking over when you're away, but you're the one who makes things move. The more moving you do, the more money you make, the more bonus I get. QED – glad to have you back."

"Hope you still think that in a few weeks. Right, see you tomorrow. I've a meeting first thing, so won't be in until about twelve and will need to leave by four, I would think." That would give him time to listen to Vairi, hopefully speak to her after her show, get some sleep, and still be capable of meeting Kenny for their final tidy up. Before then picking Vairi up, eating and settling down for the start of the rest of his – and hopefully their – life. "A nice shoe-in before I'm up and running."

Alberto looked at him and laughed. "There's never a time when you are not up and running. Believe me, I know. I'm the one always trying to catch you."

Nice sentiments, but the only running he felt like doing had nothing to do with work. By the time he sat in his lounge, curtains and windows open to enjoy the last evening light with a whisky – a fine Highland Park eighteen-year-old single malt this time – in his hand, he wasn't so sure. He swirled the amber liquid and smiled to himself as he remembered a heated argument with an American friend over the difference between Bourbon whiskey with an 'E' in the word, and Scotch Whisky – no 'E'. Why on earth people thought they were the same drink, he had no idea. They were about the same as rum and gin. Alcohol, and there the similarity ended. It had been a very drunken evening as both whisky and whiskey had been drunk in copious amounts to assure themselves of the differences.

Raig shook his head in amusement at his memories, finished his whisky and headed indoors to turn on the radio and listen. His phone beeped with an incoming message.

Don't forget to switch on to me.

No chance of that. His fingers flew over the keyboard.

My new, hard, and fast rule.

Ohh, hard and slow, please.

Your words are my command.

Good. Gotta go. Look forward to trying out your new rule later.

Now what exactly did she mean by that? There was no time to find out. The opening music began, and he found himself leaning forward in his seat, as if he would be able to hear better and remembered the last time he did exactly the same action.

"Good evening, listeners. Midweek Midnight with Cracking Carry C. A brilliant show for you tonight. Somewhat different than usual, in that there are no email invites. So let's have some music, then I'll tell you all about it." Her voice faded, and the melodious tones of Paul Simon singing *Fifty Ways to Leave Your Lover* took over.

Oh ho, that didn't sound too good. He poured himself another whisky without his customary addition of the same amount of water and settled to wait for the end of the song. His palms were sweaty and his pulse irregular. Shit, for years he hadn't known what sweaty palms were, not even in the stickiest of situations, and now twice in a few days. *Calm down, Raig,* he told himself. *Wait to see what she has to say.* Surely she wouldn't be so cruel as to give him his marching orders over the airwaves? No, she wasn't like that. If it was over, she would tell him face-to-face. If he gave her the chance.

"Now, peeps. Tonight is different. A lot different actually. I'm talking about trust again. Not yours, mine. Or rather, my lack of it. My stupidity. How I almost lost my lover. Without using any of those fifty ways we've just heard about, but because I didn't have trust. I expected it, got very shirty when I felt I didn't get it. But did I give it in return? Oh no, not me. Cracking Carry C kept a great big bit of her life to herself. My lover found out about my program by chance and recognized my voice. Still he wanted me, to be with me and to be part of my life. Me? I was a moron. So here's the next bit of music. Ignore all the words, just listen to the title, and substitute my name."

He laughed so hard he spilled his drink as Jilted John and *Gordon is a Moron* came across loud and clear. She really had trawled the archives for those songs.

"Yes, well" — her voice was wry — "that was me, folks. The moron. I wasn't jilted, but boy, was I stupid. The most wonderful man omitted to tell me something so immaterial, and I took a hissy fit."

Raig wasn't sure he really was hearing that. Immaterial? Wonderful? What next? What next was better. Much better.

"He loves me, really loves me. I love him and wouldn't admit it. Too up my own you-know-what, I know best and all that rubbish, and spat the dummy out. I felt something should be really important and got snotty when he didn't. Why should I be right and him wrong? Oh, idiot or what? All he asked was for me to trust him, and he would tell me everything as soon as he could. You've got it, I was noncommittal. Letting my past mess up my future. Then I had the lightbulb moment."

Blinded by the Light by Manfred Mann's Earth Band blasted his eardrums.

Raig itched to text or email, but he kept his hands firmly wrapped around his glass. He wondered what would happen next.

"As I said, lightbulb moment. I wasn't blinded by the light. I was blinded by lack of trust, but I couldn't find a track saying that. So I guess this is my way of groveling. Hoping it's not too late to say I trust you, I believe in you and I love you. You don't have to tell me things you shouldn't."

The James Bond theme came next. Raig was hopeful. Very hopeful. Full of love and admiration *for* his love. She had told the world how she felt, and he was humbled.

His phone beeped for an incoming text.

Forgive me? I didn't know how else to show you how I love and trust you. I don't need to wait until tomorrow to be with you. Any chance of a lift home? To your home?

There was an easy answer to that.

My pleasure. To our *home?*

To our home.

He was so glad he'd spilled his second whisky and not drank it. A single malt from the highlands shouldn't be wasted but this was one occasion he didn't mind.

As he grabbed shoes and a jacket, he still listened to the radio to see what else she might say.

Her voice was light, happy-sounding, full of laughter. "Please, peeps, don't get the idea he is a spy, nothing further from the truth."

Ouch.

"He's loyal, kind, true and part of me. And I love him. So this is for you, my love. Elton John and *Your Song*. From me with love."

Sheesh. There was a facer.

He grabbed the car keys, locked up the house, got into his car and drove, listening to her love and trust in words and music. Hoped and prayed it would sustain and stay strong and true after the following night. The last thing he wanted to do was break this new, precious, fragile link they had forged. He was horribly afraid that he might do so.

Chapter Fifteen

He didn't go into the station, because he didn't want to meet Stevie or anyone else. Just Vairi. He sat outside for the last few minutes of her show, enjoying the music, reveling in the sound of her voice. As the end music faded and her voice finished talking, he sent a text to tell her he was parked at the door.

Ten minutes.

It was less. He saw her leave the building, Stevie with her, and got out of the car. The air was still, the night calm with that hint of earthiness that comes with the midnight of summer. Somewhere close he could smell roses and knew he would forever associate their scent with the memory of that moment, as he watched Vairi walk to him, all the love and trust she had spoken about showing on her face for him to see.

He leaned in to her and held her tight, hardly registering Stevie leaving. He was surrounded by her presence, drowning willingly in it, oblivious to all else as he handed her into the car, walked rapidly around to the driver's side and got in. She leaned across the space between them and half slid on top of him. His cock registered her rapidly and dramatically, making her wriggle against him eagerly.

"Mmm, that's nice to feel how pleased you are to see me, touch me. Ouch, damn gearstick. How dare it think it can take the place of you?" She moved to kiss him and purred deep in her throat. "God, Raig, I have so missed you. If nothing else, my stupidity had done one thing—made me accept how much I need you. Take me home. Your home."

"*Our* home," he corrected gently with a mental prayer — *I hope.*

She slung a shoulder bag the size of a small suitcase onto the backseat. He looked at it, then her, a question in his eyes.

She must have read and interpreted it correctly. "I hoped," she said simply.

What had he done to deserve all this? To deserve her? *F-all, that's what,* he thought morosely. *F-bloody-all.* So much was riding on the following evening. Before that, they had the rest of this night — well, day, he corrected himself as he looked at the clock on the dashboard. Oh shit, hell, and other epithets he could think of. No, they didn't.

"Love, I need to work tomorrow. Tie up some loose ends and things like that. Will you be fine?"

She squeezed his thigh, sending his cock on high alert. "I'm a big girl. I can entertain myself, although I do prefer you to do it. For goodness' sake, love, I've got a book and my knitting. Think I'll knit a willy warmer for you." She laughed and rolled her eyes, probably at the look of horror he knew he had on his face. "Stop worrying. Everything will be fine. I told you, hell, I told however many thousand listeners, I love you and trust you. Whatever you want to say tomorrow — no, tonight — there is no need. Unless you *are* an ax murderer, of course. Then I do want to know. Make sure there are no axes about."

"No, Vairi My Queen, not that." Maybe worse? "It will be all explained tonight, I promise."

"You don't have to, Raig. I mean what I say. I. Trust. You. I. Love. You. Okay?"

"Okay, but we'll still wait until tonight for you to decide if I am really who you want to be with." Through the windscreen, he watched the Tarmac stretching into the distance, moonlight shining down on its seeming smoothness, showing all its imperfections. *A bit like me,* he thought. Nothing wrong showing up until you shine a spotlight. Pinning your hopes and dreams on something so big. That's the price to pay.

She shifted in her seat to look at him. "What exactly do you mean by that?" The tone had danger running through it loud and clear. "We have the rest of this night. Do we not?"

Ah, crunch time again. "Not. Not until you know all about me."

"*What?*" The screech could have shattered glass at twenty-five paces. Thank God for reinforced windscreens.

"I'm not making love to you until you know the real me," he said, stubborn to the last. "I'm going to do the right thing for once."

"Stop the car."

"What?"

"Stop the bloody car. *Now.*" She thumped his thigh as she spoke.

With a quick look in the rearview mirror, he indicated and pulled into the curb.

"Right. What the fuck is going on? And stop bloody thumping me." He grabbed her hands and held them firm. "Right, why the freak out? I'm being the good guy here. Not taking advantage of you."

"Argh. No." She shook her head. "I want you to take advantage of me. I want you naked in me, making me scream your name. You, you…"

Obviously, he thought, bemused, *she can't find a word bad enough.*

"You twerp. What's the point of going all noble now?" She pulled their hands down together to rest on the hard, pulsing ridge under his zip. "I want you, you want me. Where's the problem?"

"No, not until you know me. *Then* I will make love to you, not before."

Her eyes narrowed. "So, you're saying you won't make love to me until after this great, big this-is-me thing goes down?"

He nodded, wary.

She smiled, a deep, sultry, sensuous, suspicious smile. "No problem, then. Carry on driving."

He started the car. And nearly ran into the ditch.

"I'll make love to you. You can lie back and grin and bear it. *Mind the tree.*"

Mind the tree. After a statement like that, she was lucky they weren't out of the car and against the tree. He concentrated on the road ahead. Not on his cock, agreeing with everything she said, or on her soft breath. Definitely not on her hand resting on his thigh, her fingers occasionally brushing his jeans over where said cock pulsed. Never had thirty miles seemed so long. Even his drive, which, with its satisfying crunch of gravel, gave him a feeling of coming home when he drove over it, seemed four miles, not one.

By the time he'd activated the garage door and driven inside, he was hard pressed not to put her seat back and dive inside her warmth. Two things stopped him—the fact he was determined not to make love to her before she heard everything, and if he was honest, the realization he was excited and aroused by the thoughts of how she might make love to him. To say nothing of the fact he was too damn old to negotiate a gearstick that wasn't part of him!

Instead, he carefully, painfully walked around the car to open her door and help her out. Chivalry darned well wasn't dead, even if she only laughed and used his hand to lever herself against him. Automatically he moved against her.

She slapped his butt, none too gently.

"Uh-uh, you're not going to make love to me, remember? Everything that happens will be instigated and activated by me. Only me. You, my love, will lie back and suffer."

She took hold of both his hands. He could, if he had chosen, easily moved them, but he didn't choose to.

"Or enjoy," she said conversationally, before continuing in the same tone. "Is there anyone in the house waiting for us?"

He shook his head. "Nope. My housekeeper doesn't live

in. She has that cottage at the bottom of the drive. Why?"

"I just wondered. No, I'll get it," she told him as he reached for her bag. "Lead on."

She had something in mind, he'd bet on it. His own mind began to race over possibilities as he opened the door from the garage to the house and turned off the alarm. *Kitchen table? The stairs? The Jacuzzi*—no, he discarded that since Vairi didn't know about it. *Wait and see, Raig.*

Or…not see!

He found a soft, silken cover blocking out his sight. Registered the door latched behind him and the sound of a key turning.

"Stand there." Her voice was soft and hesitant. Not so self-assured then. He nodded and waited, listening. He could hear doors opening and closing, the sound of footsteps on the stairs. It was a strange feeling, to be vulnerable, to be able to listen and not see. He mentally gave thanks for the gift of sight.

He was so immersed in his thoughts he almost missed her return. It was that all-important prickle of awareness that had him turning in her direction before he heard the footsteps. At least he thought it was her. Nothing else sent messages through his cock and balls like her presence.

Smooth hands remove his jacket. Raig shivered as soft breaths whispered over his skin and gentle breathing, sounded in his ear. Still in his dark world, his other senses were on high alert. Somehow he knew she was standing in front of him and just looking at him. His hands stretched out of their own volition. The air around him was displaced by a swirl of movement. Something soft was firmly attached to his left wrist. He tugged and caught her laugh.

"I told you I was a Girl Guide. I passed all my knot badges." His hand was moved behind his back and tied to the other one before he stopped her. Not that he had any intention of doing so, this assault on his senses was bloody arousing.

"Now, you trust me not to let you bump into anything or

fall over?" Her voice was full of humor. "First though." His mouth was assaulted in the best way possible as she moved her tongue over his teeth, demanded entrance then danced around inside, meshing and teasing. His fingers found his nipples—he had no idea when his shirt had been opened and his chest laid bare for her to touch and explore.

"I'm leading you now," she said finally as her mouth slowly left his. He felt them move to the left. Not upstairs then? Maybe the kitchen was right. Suddenly he found himself being twirled around in a circle. By the time he was steadied again, he had no idea which direction he was facing and said so.

"That's the idea. Otherwise, where's the element of surprise? Now I can keep you guessing." Once again, a hand on his shoulder was guiding him, he thought, across the hallway. What next? He didn't have a clue and was excited by the notion.

"Stand there a sec." He heard a noise as if a chair was being moved, then the sound and feel of his zip being lowered followed by the scrape of denim moving down his legs and cool, refreshing air caressing his skin. Going commando sometimes paid off, even when the only reason you had done it was to get out of the house in a hurry.

"Right, just behind you. Sit down slowly." He complied and almost yelped as a cold, hard seat met his overheated body.

"Fuck, that's cold," he muttered as he perched gingerly on the chilly surface. "Is this to deflate me?"

"Oh hell, sorry." *She doesn't sound all that sorry*, he thought wryly as his body adjusted to the temperature cocooning his ass. She sounded gleeful. "I want you to be easily accessible."

Huh? "Er, um, pardon, my love? I'm butt naked, as far as I can tell. If that's not easily accessible, I don't know what is. What about you? Are you butt naked and accessible as well?"

She purred, no other word for it, and he felt her breasts

against his chest, her nipples touching him. "Well now, that's immaterial, isn't it? Because you aren't going to touch me. This is *my* show, played out how I want it. I wonder... yes." His jeans scratched his skin as they scrunched firmly around his ankles, limiting his movements as surely as if she had tied them, and cool air teased his chest. Vairi had undone and pushed his shirt pushed down his arms to his restraints. Fuck, what was happening? She had hooked the shirt over the chair back, limiting his movements even further. His cock responded to the arousal his mind experienced and throbbed to an almost unbearable pitch.

The unexpected warmth of her mouth as it closed around him, licking and sucking, would have had him off the chair if a small hand had not held him down

"Stay," she mumbled around a mouthful of cock. She used her teeth to nip and graze along the hard length, inviting him to swell and fill as her hands tweaked and played with his rock-hard nipples and smoothed over his body with sensuous strokes. He leaned back in the chair as best he could and absorbed all she was doing, all he discerned.

Sheesh, now her teeth were grazing his balls. He felt them taken into her mouth and sucked, like she was playing with plum stones or apricots. An almost indescribable sensation built. It was the one that made him realize, hell, he was going to come.

"Vairi, shit this is amazing. Gonna come." He decided it was only fair to warn her. "So, if you don't want to drink me, now's the time to back off."

His reply was ice-cold. Literally. He yelped as a cold cube was rubbed firmly over the base of his cock.

"Not yet. Not until I decide." The inside of her mouth was chilly as she took him again. Obviously the ice cube worked in more than one place.

The heat she was generating soon warmed him. He knew nothing she could say or do was going to stop his climax. As he tensed and began to shake, her mouth gripped and moved faster and harder.

"That's it, love." Although muttered, he heard every word, felt the rumble of them run through him. "Now. Come for me now, my Rake, fuck my mouth. Come on, now. Come *now!*"

He did. Afterward, he wondered if his roar of triumph had been heard in the village. He filled her with cock and cum pumping, enjoying the way her lips tightened around him, sucking and swallowing until he was dry and shaking. Still she kept her mouth firm on his dick until he was quiescent. Slowly she moved. He wanted to hold her, to embrace her trembling and the way she cried out as he had. Not the right time, he sensed that. This had been her gift to him, and what a gift. He felt his jeans moved, his hands untied, then his eyes were uncovered and he blinked as he adjusted to the light. Vairi stood fully clothed in front of him, her eyes wary.

"That, my love, was the most beautiful, arousing, generous and fucking sexy thing I have ever experienced," Raig said huskily. "Any time you want to repeat it, I'm your man. I give in. Wholeheartedly, unreservedly. Can I take you to our bed and make love to you?" He'd worry about tonight, well, tonight. Priorities, he told himself. Priorities. The first of those was to bury himself deep inside his love.

In answer, she held out her hands to him. "I thought you'd never ask."

* * * *

By seven o'clock that evening he was antsy. After several hours of glorious lovemaking, he'd made his meeting by the skin of his teeth, having rushed to his office for it, and had told Berto not to expect him in the following day before driving home and finding Vairi sunbathing in the secret garden. In the nude, the Jacuzzi bubbling away gently behind her, inviting them to embrace its warm caress. It had certainly stopped him worrying about what was to come. But now, with only a couple of hours left, he needed to sit Vairi down and talk to her.

She was pottering about in the kitchen wearing one of his shirts, the sleeves turned up, and a smile. Nothing else. His cock, encased in his habitual jeans, albeit with no snap fastened and the zip half down, was responding as it always did to her presence. Helping to hold up said denims.

"D'you want butter with this?" She turned from the crusty loaf she was cutting. "Or is pâté enough?"

"I wouldn't mind butter with you." He put his arms around her waist from behind and moved his fingers unerringly to her clit to run and arouse. She moaned and pushed both into his fingers and back to his cock, no mean feat. "But we need to talk." He nipped her nape. The knife waved threateningly. "Pâté is fine," he added in haste. "Come and sit down in the lounge. We'll bring this with us." He grabbed the bowl of salad and the cutlery, leaving her to bring the pâté and bread.

"Right." He paused as she settled next to him. "What do you know about Mickey Dooley?"

She put her head to one side, something he had noticed she did when considering how to answer a question. "Investigative reporter, known as The Irishman." She stared at him for a long moment then a smile played over her lips. "That newspaper article I read was all about him. Brave bloke. Helped to put a fair few people away. Won awards, supposed to always be in disguise, no one knows what he looks like. Except, I guess, those he has investigated while in disguise."

"And now you."

She stared at him as if he had grown horns and a tale. "Pardon?"

He kissed her and took hold of her hand. "And now you. For a short while. I've just arranged his demise. As of nine p.m. tonight, the whole world, well, those watching the TV, on the correct channel, will know he is out of business. No more Mickey D. For those who need to know — hello, Padraig O'Shea."

"You?" Her voice was incredulous. "That's you? Bloody hell, I wondered when you asked me because of his moniker, The Irishman, but never really… Oh my God, Raig, all those dangerous things. Shit, you could have been killed before I ever knew you." She was crying, tears running down her cheeks. "Are you safe now?" Vairi took hold of his shoulders none too gently and shook him. "Please tell me you are."

"*We* are safe now, love. That's what all the cloak-and-dagger stuff was about. After the documentary, we will be safe. I wanted us to be together, see his demise and look forward to the future. Will you do that? Forgive me for the secrecy?"

In reply, she kissed him with fierce passion. "Of course I will, you moron."

"Well then, Vairi My Queen, are you ready to begin the rest of our life together? And don't give me any of that shit about the age difference. You're only —"

"As old as you feel," she finished for him. "So that makes me a youngster, and you the oldie. Oh, my pleasure, my love."

"And mine," he assured her. "Oh, and mine."

Epilogue

Nine months later

"Okay, Ma, let's get this show on the road eh?" Lorna fussed with the hem of Vairi's dress and grinned. "Before you ask, no, the bump doesn't show, yes, you do have both earrings in, no, your skirts aren't tucked into your knickers and yes, Raig is here waiting for you. Not so patiently over by the door. So get your ass into gear and join him."

Raig grinned, as Vairi swung around to glare at him.

"It's not the done thing for the groom to see the bride before the wedding, you know," she said snappily. "Why are you here?"

"Ah now then, I come in peace," he said in his best brogue as held his hands in the air in mock surrender and kept his face straight as Lorna sidled out of another exit.

"It's our wedding now. This minute — or as soon as we take the few steps into the other room. And I have something for you." Raig pushed himself off the doorjamb and sauntered toward her. "I have in my pocket a letter I believe you'll like. Something about an award I think."

"An award? You've won an award?" She whooped. "What for, when, how, who… Ooft."

Raig shut her up by hauling her to him and kissing her hard. The softness of her rounded belly pressed against him and he sighed as he deepened the kiss. Lord, how he'd waited for this moment. It had been a long six months of 'will we, won't we, what next?'

Now though before they said I do he had something even more exciting — in one way — to tell her. He lifted his lips from hers. "I haven't."

"Haven't what?" Vairi tilted her head up to look at him properly. Her eyes were still glazed with desire. Macho though it was, Raig got not a little satisfaction knowing it was he who did that to her.

"Won an award. You might have."

"Me? But... Gimme that letter! How come you got it? What does it say?" She all but danced on the spot as he hauled two envelopes out of his pocket. "What's in the other one?"

"A letter from Kenny saying that Mr. Dooley, deceased, didn't get nominated. Thank god. Now we really can put it all behind us. But I did get a list of nominees and a certain Carry C is up for best radio show and best individual program."

"Oh my. Open it for me, please. My hands are trembling, look." Vairi held her visibly shaking hands in the air. "What program?"

"The one about you and me and trust. Look." Raig took the sheet of paper out of the envelope and waved it at her. "You'll ace it."

Vairi scanned the paper and grinned at him. "Well, I couldn't have done it without you as a subject, could I? So, let's go and get married then we can celebrate this and" — she patted her tummy — "this."

It was just what Raig wanted to hear. Over the last few months they'd both had a lot to contend with. Rumors that Mickey Dooley wasn't dead — just temporarily retired. It had been a tense time as they both wondered what the hell might happen. He'd made sure Vairi was never alone, even though she argued he needed the same level of protection. They had made love each night as if it were the last time, and he had been sure she had given thanks as fervently as he when it eventually the furor had died down.

Especially as it had resulted in someone having their balls metaphorically chewed off.

Vairi's refusal of his marriage proposal until, as she said, she was sure they were both sure, hadn't really been a surprise. He still hadn't quite fathomed all of that one out — he'd always been sure. However, she'd always argued a bit of paper wasn't necessary to show their commitment to each other so he could understand her prevaricating. Even so, Raig had acknowledged he was old-fashioned enough to want everything signed, sealed and delivered. Mindful of his love's dogmatic and obstinate attitude, he hadn't pressed it though. Just hoped one day she'd let him propose then she would say yes.

They rearranged furniture so the house by the sea was to both their liking and one magical day he'd carried a giggling Vairi over the threshold, up the stairs and to their new bed. Which they'd proceeded to thoroughly christen.

Vairi had grilled him thoroughly about his ex-alter ego. Sworn at some of his near misses and praised him for his commitment. Then had said very forcefully she was glad it was all over.

"So we can live a normal life," she'd added.

Raig had kissed her nose. "Define normal. Go on, I dare you."

Vairi had wound her arms around his neck and rubbed her knickerless — but hidden by a linen skirt — pussy over his denim-covered cock. "Ah well, you have a point. Whatever we chose it to be, I guess."

A month later, as they'd were both been getting ready for a day out on the bike, Vairi had got down on her knee and said oh-so-seriously. "Padraig O'Shea, will you marry me?"

Raig — commando as they both preferred — had been in the middle of zipping up his jeans. He'd sworn as he caught the soft flesh of his cock in between the teeth of the zip.

Vairi's eyes had widened as she'd seen what had happened. "No, don't mutilate yourself. It's not that bad, honestly."

"Idiot." Raig had eased the metal away from his dick. It had been a close shave with very little between a bruise plus a lack of nooky for a week and a simple 'ouch, be careful'.

"Are you sure?"

"That it's not that bad?' she'd asked with a wicked grin on her face. "Of course I am."

"Vairi, love, seriously…" It had been nigh on impossible to put into words what he was trying to ask her. Luckily, he hadn't needed to explain further.

"Seriously, my Raig, I want to marry you. Here in our home, with the sea as our music and the garden as our church. When we should get good weather and a chance to dance under the stars, when everyone else has gone home. Celebrate how bloody lucky we are."

That he hoped was about to happen. "How's bump?" Raig asked as he watched, amused, as Vairi smoothed her hair back and did her ineffectual best to tuck the three errant curls that had a mind of their own into the complicated knot at the nape of her neck. "No, leave them, love. They're you, me and bump makes three."

Vairi giggled. "Oh, you. Okay. I'm ready. Do you think anyone suspects bump is now a fine three-month-old secret inside me?"

Rig patted her almost-showing bump and bent his head. "There, there, bump, my love. Mummy and Daddy are being selfish and not sharing you yet." He straightened. "Who cares? I'd love to shout it from the top of the hills, but I want to savor our secret as well."

"Yeah, so…" She straightened his tie and went on tip-toe to kiss the top of his head. "Shall we go and get married then?"

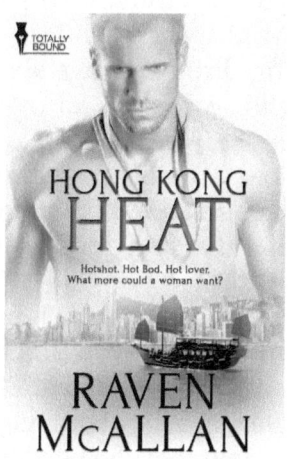

Hong Kong Heat

Excerpt

Chapter One

And hey, Hong Kong is as great as I remember. I can't wait to get out and explore. This hotel lives up to everything it boasts about. My suite is amazing and the bed is big enough for an orgy.

Debra considered the last sentence then deleted it. It might be a bit too much for her children to read.

Everyone is so helpful and friendly. And wow, you should have seen the hot-bod guy in the foyer. Pity he'd disappeared once I'd checked in. (Only kidding, I don't cradle snatch, but my eyes are still 20/20.) Ah well, lots to do and see. Speak soon, love mum x

Debra checked that she'd copied the email to both of her adult children and pressed send. No doubt if Lena were there she would roll her eyes and mutter things about safe sex and growing old gracefully, then giggle and high five her mum. Kevan would worry and ask if she had a rape alarm, before issuing dire warnings about insurances and idiot old people who wandered all over the world. Such different attitudes.

Debra wasn't *old* old — merely past the mid-life crisis age. Not that her children agreed with that description. To them it was a mid-life crisis that had gone on a bit too long.

Tough.

Deb knew why she'd resolved to do her gap year at the ripe old age of forty-four. Her beloved husband Don had died five years earlier and she'd wallowed. Then floundered.

Until she'd read an article about gap year oldies and understood immediately that she needed to be one.

So here she was in Hong Kong, in an exclusive Channing Hotel and wondering just who the man she'd spotted was.

Too young for me is what he was. Ah well. Debra checked that she'd got everything she might need in her bag, picked up her room key and sunglasses and plotted her route in her mind.

Hong Kong.

Somewhere she hadn't been for years and one of her favorite cities in the world. It had been a conscious choice to leave it until she was on her way home. A final glorious ending to a year of wandering the world, before she headed back to Scotland. She had almost two weeks to relearn her way around and decide where on the islands was her favorite spot, and she wasn't going to waste a second.

First, she was going to check out the rooftop terrace and swimming pool. It had been one of the things that had influenced her choice of hotels. That and the reputation of Channing Hotels.

The lift was speedy and within seconds it seemed that she was smiling at the pool attendant and wandering around a well-tended garden in the sky.

Debra walked amongst shrubs and flowers and admired the views. In one direction was the park she wanted to visit.

Its trees looked like toys made out of plasticine and the people walking through it like ants. In the other she could see the harbor with one of the famous green Star Ferries crossing to TST, a junk picking up litter and a cruise liner in dock. She took in a deep breath. She loved it.

Considering that Hong Kong was a skyscraper paradise, this area was remarkably empty of multistoried buildings. The hotel was the tallest around even though it merely had twenty or so floors. That meant that the gardens, pool and a well thought out walking track were not overlooked. It was peaceful and private and, at that moment, unused. Debra made a note to use it all as soon as she could.

But not now. Now the streets and park beckoned. She made her way downstairs.

The foyer was empty except for two doormen, one who held the door open, and the other who bowed.

"Taxi, ma'am?"

Debra shook her head. "No thanks. I'm off for a wander around the park."

The doorman smiled. "Enjoy your walk, ma'am. Best time of day for it, I reckon."

"I think so. Thank you." The exchange reminded her how pleasant most people were. She stood at the door and debated which way to go. It was still warm, very warm, although luckily without the humidity that would hit the city in a few weeks' time.

The streets were busy. Businessmen and women, teens in school uniforms, toddlers and their carers. Some rushed, others sauntered or stood chatting.

It was time for the commuting nightmare that occurred every weekday at that time. People of all shapes and sizes were about. Nowhere could she see one specific tall-haired man in a sharp suit and crisp white shirt. Debra was surprised at the stab of annoyance and disappointment that hit her. After all, she'd merely glimpsed the guy as she'd followed the concierge and her luggage to reception. Why would he be in this crowded street?

But that glimpse made me want more. Grief, I'm getting old if one tiny sighting makes me go weak at the knees. Snap out of it.

Pleased with her self-lecture, Debra put on her sunglasses, thankful that she'd slathered herself in sun cream before she'd left her suite, and headed for Victoria Park. The last time she'd been there you couldn't see the grass for the hundreds of au pairs, Amahs, Ayis and immigrant workers who spent their day off sitting in the park and chatting. The noise level would have won out over any pop concert. Today it was quieter, with a few children playing ball, a group of elderly ladies talking as they enjoyed the late afternoon sunshine and several people using the jogging track that circled part of the park.

She found an area of grass in the sunshine and settled down on it to read about her latest sex on legs hero and how he managed to convince his lady that he wanted her. Within minutes, Debra was engrossed. As a child she'd often been chastised for being oblivious to everything other than her book when she was reading.

Today was no exception. It wasn't until the sun moved behind the trees and she was sitting in the shade that Debra realized how much time had passed.

The occupants of the park had changed. To one side, a tai chi lesson was in process and the jogging track was much busier. Debra checked her watch and groaned. She'd been oblivious for well over an hour and undoubtedly ought to move and think about getting ready for dinner.

Getting up wasn't as easy as she'd hoped. Sitting in one position for so long had given her pins and needles and she winced at the pain.

I don't mind nice stings and tingles, well I didn't, but hey, it's been so long, who knows? But this is bloody agony. She rubbed her legs and wriggled her toes to get the circulation back to normal.

Debra collected her belongings and made her way across the grass towards the entrance to the park. To get there she had to cross the jogging track and dodge the joggers.

Their numbers had increased considerably now and Debra waited to let a steady stream of people of all shapes and sizes go by. One guy, tall, fit and blond hair, caught her eye and her heart did a weird double pitter pat.

It was the guy from the hotel. No snazzy suit, but black running shorts and a black sleeveless vest that shouted serious runner to her. As he approached along the track, she couldn't help but admire—and drool at—the way he moved. His short hair had curled in the heat and the sheen of sweat over his body highlighted the muscles in his arms and the strength of his legs. She'd bet he had a washboard stomach and a cute ass.

More books from
Totally Bound Publishing

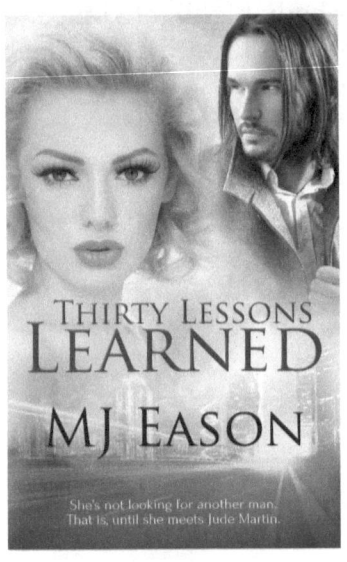

Experience has shown Paige Wilder that relationships end badly, so she's not looking for another. That is, until she meets Jude Martin.

Book two in the Souls Entwined series

Unexpected passions will tempt two lovers – body, heart and soul…

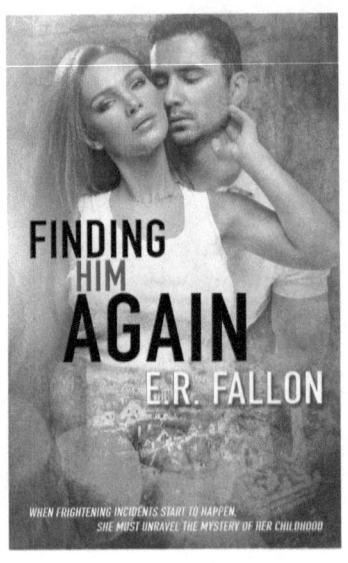

She came home to find the one romance she always
regretted not having…

The world has its empty places, and so does the heart.

About the Author

Raven McAllan

A multi-published author of erotic romance, Raven lives in Scotland, along with her husband and their two cats — their children having flown the nest — surrounded by beautiful scenery, which inspires a lot of the settings in her books.

She is used to sharing her life with the occasional deer, red squirrel, and lost tourist, to say nothing of the scourge of Scotland — the midge. As once she is writing she is oblivious to everything else, her lovely long-suffering husband is learning to love the dust bunnies, work the Aga, and be on stand-by with a glass of wine.

Raven McAllan loves to hear from readers. You can find contact information, website details and an author profile page at https://www.totallybound.com/

TOTALLY
BOUND

Home of Erotic Romance